"I'd better get you home, Kitten."

"Kitten?"

Sam smiled. "You remind me of one," he explained gently. "You're all soft and cuddly."

"I have claws," Marjorie warned.

Again he smiled. "Now that's something I can personally attest to."

Marjorie grinned at him as she collected her jacket and purse. She paused in the entryway. "It seems I'm always in your debt. First you rescue me from the jaws of death..."

"That's a slight exaggeration."

"Then you buy a car from me..."

"One I intended to purchase anyway."

"Next, you feed me." Marjorie's trusting brown eyes were gazing into his.

And there was a lot more he would be interested in doing for her, Sam thought, if she didn't hurry up and leave....

Dear Reader:

The spirit of the Silhouette Romance Homecoming Celebration lives on as each month we bring you six books by continuing stars!

And there are some wonderful stories in the stars for you. During the coming months, we're publishing romances by many of your favorite authors, including Brittany Young, Lucy Gordon and Rita Rainville. In addition, we have some very special treats planned for the fall and winter of 1988.

In October, watch for *Tyler*—Book III of Diana Palmer's exciting trilogy, Long, Tall Texans. Diana's handsome Tyler is sure to lasso your heart—forever!

Also in October is Annette Broadrick's *Come Be My Love*—the exciting sequel to *That's What Friends Are For*. Remember Greg Duncan, the mysterious bridegroom? Well, sparks fly when he meets his match—Brandi Martin!

And Sal Giordiano, the handsome detective featured in *Sherlock's Home* by Sharon De Vita, is returning in November with his own story—*Italian Knights*.

There's plenty more for you to discover in the Silhouette Romance line during the fall and winter. So as the weather turns colder, enjoy the warmth of love while you are reading Silhouette Romances. Your response to these authors and other authors of Silhouette Romances has served as a touchstone for us, and we're pleased to bring you more books with Silhouette's distinctive medley of charm, wit and—above all—*romance*.

I hope you enjoy this book and the many stories to come. Come home to Silhouette Romance—for always!

Sincerely,

Tara Hughes
Senior Editor
Silhouette Books

DEBBIE MACOMBER

Any Sunday

Silhouette *Romance*

Published by Silhouette Books New York

America's Publisher of Contemporary Romance

To Darlene Layman for her loyal friendship
and her unselfish efforts for RWA in Region 4

Special thanks to
Pat Thiessen and Brad Pederson,
Mercedes salesmen for Doxon Motors,
Tacoma, Washington

SILHOUETTE BOOKS
300 E. 42nd St., New York, N.Y. 10017

ISBN: 0-373-08603-2

First Silhouette Books printing September 1988

Printed in the U.S.A.

Books by Debbie Macomber

Silhouette Romance

That Wintry Feeling #316
Promise Me Forever #341
Adam's Image #349
The Trouble with Caasi #379
A Friend or Two #392
Christmas Masquerade #405
Shadow Chasing #415
Yesterday's Hero #426
Laughter in the Rain #437
Jury of His Peers #449
Yesterday Once More #461
Friends—and Then Some #474
Sugar and Spice #494
No Competition #512
Love 'n' Marriage #522
Mail-Order Bride #539
*Cindy and the Prince #555
*Some Kind of Wonderful #567
*Almost Paradise #579
Any Sunday #603

*Legendary Lovers trilogy

Silhouette Special Edition

Starlight #128
Borrowed Dreams #241
Reflections of Yesterday #284
White Lace and Promises #322
All Things Considered #392

Silhouette Christmas Stories 1986

"Let it Snow"

DEBBIE MACOMBER

has quickly become one of Silhouette's most prolific authors. As a wife and mother of four, she not only manages to keep her family happy, but she also keeps her publisher and readers happy with each book she writes.

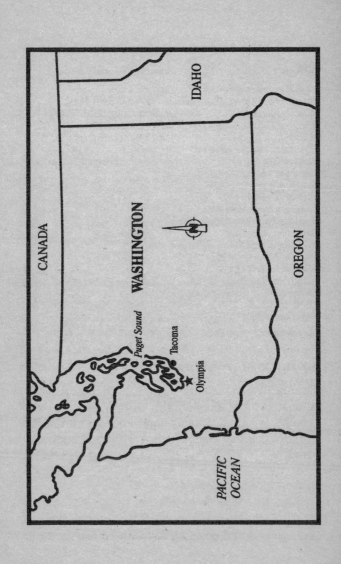

Chapter One

Marjorie Majors's deep brown eyes widened as a flash of burning pain shot through her side. Feeling hot and flushed again, she guessed she was running a fever. Her smile was decidedly forced as she walked across the showroom floor, weaving her way around the shiny new Mercedes while lightly pressing her hand against her hipbone. Maybe if she ignored the throbbing ache, this unexplained malady would vanish on its own. Her reasoning hadn't worked, though, and the mysterious discomfort had persisted for days.

"Is your side hurting you again?" Lydia Mason, the title and license clerk for Dixon Motors, called from behind the front counter.

"A little." Now that had to be the understatement of the week, Marjorie mused. The shooting pain had been coming and going all day with no real rhyme or reason. Marjorie should have known she wasn't going to be able to fool Lydia. Her friend had a nose for news. Little transpired at Dixon Motors without Lydia knowing about it.

"Honestly, Marjorie, why don't you just see a doctor?"

"I'm fine," she protested. "Besides, I don't have a doctor."

Lydia, who stood barely five feet tall and wore heels that swelled her height an additional three inches, moved around the counter. Her mouth was pinched into a tight line of determination. "But you haven't been feeling good all week."

"Has it been that long?"

"Longer, I suspect," Lydia murmured, shaking her head. "Listen, no one is going to think less of you for needing a doctor, for heaven's sake. Just because you're the only female salesperson here, that doesn't mean you have to behave like Joan of Arc."

"But it's just a little tummy ache."

"What did you have for lunch?"

Marjorie shrugged noncommittally, preferring not to lie. A wry smile lifted the corners of her full mouth as she pretended to survey the parking lot, hoping a prospective buyer would magically appear so she'd have an excuse to drop the conversation. She didn't want to admit that with her stomach acting up, she hadn't bothered to eat lunch. And now that she thought about it, breakfast hadn't appealed to her, either.

"You didn't have any lunch, did you?" Lydia challenged.

"I didn't have time since . . ."

"That's it, Marjorie—that's the final straw. I'm making you an appointment with my gynecologist."

"You're what?"

"You heard me." Lydia didn't wait for an argument. With her manicured fingernails, she flipped the hair that had fallen across her cheek to the back of her shoulder and marched around the counter with the authority of a marine drill sergeant.

"Don't call a gynecologist! That's crazy. I don't need a woman's doctor—an internist maybe . . ."

Ignoring Marjorie's protest, Lydia pressed the telephone receiver to her ear and turned her back to her friend. "What's crazy," Lydia said, twisting her head around, her eyes sparking with impatience, "is suffering for days because you're afraid to see a doctor."

"I am not afraid! And a gynecologist is the last person I want to see." Marjorie couldn't seem to get it through her friend's thick skull that a queasy stomach was unworthy of all this fuss. From the way Lydia was behaving, Marjorie fully expected her friend to dial 911 to report a minor pain that came and went without warning. She'd lived with it for the last few days—a little longer wasn't going to matter. More than likely it would disappear as quickly and unexpectedly as it had come. Or so she hoped.

"Today, if possible." Lydia spoke firmly into the telephone. She placed her hand over the receiver and turned to Marjorie. "Listen, I had a friend once with similar symptoms and it ended up being female problems and—'' She broke off abruptly. ''Five o'clock would be fine. Thanks, Mary.''

Although Marjorie knew it wouldn't do any good, she tried again. ''Lydia...''

The telephone was replaced in its cradle before Lydia turned around. ''And something else. Dr. Sam isn't your run-of-the-mill doctor! He's wonderful! If you need to see someone else, he'll refer you, so stop looking so worried.''

''But I'm not sure this pain is anything.''

''Then checking it out won't be any big deal. Right?''

Marjorie shrugged.

''He has an opening this afternoon at five.''

''His name is Dr. Sam?'' Now Marjorie had heard everything. ''Will Nurse Jane be there, too?''

''He's really terrific,'' Lydia announced with a loud sigh, obviously choosing to ignore Marjorie's sarcasm. ''I think I fell in love with him in the delivery room just before Jimmy was born. He was so gentle and understanding when I was in labor. He made me feel like I was the most noble, heroic woman in the world for enduring the pain of childbirth.''

''Hey, I've got a bit of a stomachache. I'm not looking to find Prince Charming.''

''But he's handsome, too.''

''Does Dr. Sam have another name?'' She wasn't traumatized by the thought of seeing a physician, but the simple truth was that Marjorie hated relying on anyone else. She could take care of herself very well

and relying on another person went against her fiercely
independent nature.

"His name is really Sam Bretton, but everyone calls
him Dr. Sam."

Marjorie rolled her eyes toward the ceiling. "I don't
know if I can trust a man who sounds like he keeps
office on Sesame Street."

"Wait and see," Lydia claimed, writing out direc-
tions to the medical center on a piece of paper and
ripping it free of the tablet before handing it over to
Marjorie. "He's marvelous—trust me."

Marjorie folded the paper in half and stuck it inside her purse. If nothing else, it would be interesting
to meet the guy. Lydia wasn't generally free with
praise, and according to her, this physician was another Walter Reed.

"You'll like him, I promise," Lydia added.

Marjorie made a barely perceptible movement of
her head, as if to say it made no difference to her how
she felt about him. She didn't care what he looked like
as long as he could give her something for this blasted
pain.

At precisely ten minutes to five Marjorie pulled into
the parking lot of the large medical complex north of
Tacoma General Hospital. The ache that had troubled her most of the day had vanished, just as she
knew it would, and she generally felt better. If she'd
had a fever earlier, she was convinced it was gone now.
Briefly she toyed with the idea of heading back to her
apartment and forgetting the whole thing, but that

would be irresponsible, and if Marjorie knew anything, it was the meaning of responsibility. Besides, her co-worker would be furious with her for canceling at the last moment.

Two other women were seated in the waiting room. Both were in the advanced stages of pregnancy. One sat with her hands resting on her protruding belly, looking content, while the other knit. The thick needles, encased in a pastel shade of yarn, moved furiously. Their smiles were friendly as Marjorie stepped up to the reception desk to announce her arrival. An older, gray-haired woman handed Marjorie a questionnaire and asked her to fill out several forms.

Marjorie took the clipboard and located a seat in the corner beside a dying houseplant. The yellowish leaves did little to boost her confidence in this unknown physician.

"Is this the first time you've seen Dr. Sam?" one of the soon-to-be-mothers asked.

Marjorie nodded and slipped the pen behind the clip. "My friend recommended him."

"He's absolutely wonderful."

"And good-looking to boot," the knitter added.

"Real good-looking!"

The two pregnant women eyed each other and shared a smile. "I suppose all women fall in love with their doctors," the woman with the knitting needles commented, "but I've never known a man who's as caring as Dr. Sam is."

"I'm not pregnant." Marjorie didn't know why she felt it was necessary to tell them that. This physician may do wonders with mothers-to-be, but all Marjorie cared about was his expertise with sharp, persistent pains.

"You don't have to be pregnant," the two were quick to assure her.

"Good." Marjorie completed the information sheet and returned it to the receptionist, then subtly glanced at her watch. She hadn't experienced any real discomfort in hours and was beginning to feel like a phony. Again, the thought of skipping out of the appointment sprang to mind. Sheer stupidity, of course. If nothing else, it would be interesting to stick around and meet this doctor who seemed to be a paragon of virtue. From what Lydia and the two patients in the waiting room had said, Dr. Sam Bretton was a cross between Don Johnson and Mother Teresa.

"It'll only be a few minutes," the receptionist told her.

"No problem," Marjorie answered softly, wondering if the woman had read her mind.

A few minutes turned out to be fifteen. Marjorie was escorted into a small cubicle by a nurse who dressed as though she were shooting a scene from a popular, daytime soap opera. Her gray hair was perfectly styled in a bouffant, and even after a full day in the office, not a single strand was out of place.

Marjorie stopped just inside the room, her mind whirling. She'd been in her teens when she'd last seen a physician. Over the years there'd been minor bouts with the flu and a bad cold now and again, but overall she'd been incredibly healthy. There may have been times she should have seen a physician and hadn't, mainly because she wasn't particularly fond of anyone poking around her body, but usually she could take care of herself just fine.

"Go ahead and have a seat," the nurse instructed, gesturing toward the upholstered examination table.

Reluctantly Marjorie walked into the room and pressed her backside against the oblong examining table, her elbows resting on top of the padded cover. She crossed her ankles as though she posed this way regularly, hoping to give the picture of utter nonchalance. Chagrined, she realized she'd failed miserably.

Thankfully the nurse didn't seem to notice. "What seems to be the problem?"

Marjorie shrugged. "A little pain in my side. I'm sure it's nothing."

"We'll let Dr. Sam decide that." She pulled out a thermometer and, before Marjorie could protest, stuck it under her tongue. Motioning with her hand, the nurse told Marjorie to sit on the end of the table and skillfully took her blood pressure.

"Go ahead and get undressed," she said afterward. She leaned over and pulled a paper gown from a cupboard. "When you've finished, put this on. The doctor will be with you in a couple of minutes." She left, quietly closing the door.

Marjorie mumbled disparagingly to herself as she pulled the paper gown over her head and sighed with disgust when the opening for her arm hung far wider than necessary. Keeping her arms tucked close to her side for fear the gown would reveal the sides of her breasts, she wrapped the tissue sheet around her waist and sat on the end of the paper-lined examination table. The whole idea of introducing herself to a man when she was nude felt ridiculous. All right, so he was a physician, but all that stood between her body and this stranger was a piece of tissue that felt as though a big sneeze would destroy it.

Her bare feet dangled and she kicked at the air aimlessly. The brilliant red toenails looked funny, and Marjorie absently decided to change the color. Next time she'd use a more subdued shade.

Just when she had convinced herself she was wasting her time, a polite knock sounded at the door. The knob twisted, and Marjorie painted a welcoming smile on her lips, doing her best to swallow the panic that gripped her so unexpectedly.

Dr. Sam Bretton entered the examination room, reading Marjorie's chart, his wide brow furrowed as he took in the information listed.

The first thing Marjorie noticed was his stature. Five foot seven in her stocking feet, she'd never considered herself short, but this man dwarfed her. His shoulders were broad and fit his height. His chest was deep. He wore his hair short, and his sideburns were clipped neatly around his ears. A few strands of gray at his temple provided a distinguished, sophisticated touch. He was good-looking—not strikingly handsome, but attractive enough to give credence to Lydia and the other women's claims. His eyes were a deep, dark shade of brown and the gentlest Marjorie had ever seen in a man. For an instant they mesmerized her into speechlessness. A stethoscope hung from his neck and rested against his broad, muscled chest.

"Ms. Majors." Sam smiled at his patient. Mary, his receptionist, had come to him and asked about fitting this young woman into his already-tight schedule. A friend of Lydia Mason's, Mary had said, and Sam had agreed because he was fond of Lydia. Later he'd regretted the impulse. His day had started early, and he was tired, but with one look at the wide, frightened eyes of the woman sitting on the examination table he realized he'd made the right decision. Rarely had he seen a more expressive pair of brown eyes. Marjorie Majors was as nervous as a young mother and struggling valiantly to disguise it. Her chin trembled slightly, yet she met his gaze with pride and more mettle than he'd seen in years. She resembled a lost kitten he'd once found in a rainstorm; her wide eyes were round and appealing, and it looked as though she'd turn and bolt at any moment.

"Doctor." The return of her voice brought with it the reappearance of her poise and aplomb. Her chin came up with the forced determination not to let him know how nervous she was. She handed him her business card.

He removed it from her stiff fingers, read it casually and nodded before sticking it inside the medical folder. "Your chart states that the last time you saw a physician was at age fourteen." He grimaced; whatever was bothering her now must be traumatic for her to seek professional help. A list of possibilities ran through his mind, most of them unpleasant. In the last ten years he'd seen everything.

"I had an ear infection." Marjorie pointed to her right ear with her index finger while her heart beat at double time. She was literally shaking. She couldn't understand why she should react this way. Certainly this doctor didn't frighten her. His type lent confidence, not fear.

"You're experiencing pain in your right side?"

"That's correct," Marjorie said, and her voice wobbled as she jabbered on witlessly. "I don't think it's anything to be concerned about... probably one of those common female problems. No doubt it will go away in a couple of days."

"How long has it been bothering you?"

"A week... maybe longer," she admitted reluctantly.

His thick brows contracted into a single, dark line. "Fever?"

Marjorie nodded. "But not high. It seems to be worse at night."

"Nausea? Dizziness?"

Again Marjorie answered with a nod.

"How has your back felt?"

"Sore." She wondered how he knew that. "Is that bad?" she asked hurriedly. "I mean, I can suffer with the best of them... in fact, I have a high tolerance for pain, and if you tell me it'll simply go away, I'm sure I can get through it."

"There's no need for you to do any suffering. Go ahead and lie back." He gave her his hand to guide her into a reclining position.

"Here?" She tossed a look over her shoulder at the paper-lined examination table.

He grinned. "Here."

His hand curved around her fingers, and Marjorie's grip was surprisingly tight. What the others had said was true—Dr. Sam did inspire faith. She only wished he'd stop looking at her as though she were a pathetic, scared doe caught in a hunter's trap.

"There's no need to be nervous," he said softly. "I promise not to bite."

"It's not your teeth that bother me."

He smiled again and stepped closer to the table to stand at her side. "Are you always such a wit?"

"Only when I'm forced to introduce myself to a strange man when I'm in the nude."

"Does this happen often?" Sam couldn't believe he'd asked her that. He clamped his jaw tightly. As a physician he had taken an oath to treat each patient equally, but this one struck a familiar chord, and the danger of looking upon her as a warm, desirable woman was strong.

"Meet men when I'm nude? No!"

He laughed outright at that, relieved. "I guessed as much." Carefully he lifted up the tissue sheet at her waist and placed his fingers on her abdomen, suspecting he would find rigidity and tenderness at McBurney's point—halfway between the navel and the crest of the hipbone.

"Actually I've been feeling better the last couple of hours," Marjorie said hurriedly, hoping to suggest that whatever was wrong was curing itself. His hand felt cool and soothing against her heated flesh, and Marjorie closed her eyes. However, the instant he glided his fingers to her side and pressed down, her eyes shot open at the excruciating pain searing through her like red-hot needles.

She swore loudly and jumped from the examination table. "What the hell do you think you're doing?" she shouted, her hands crossed protectively over her stomach. The agony lingered, and she nearly doubled over with the force of it.

"Miss Majors..."

"And what were all those platitudes about not needing to suffer?"

"Miss Majors, if you'd kindly return to the table."

"Are you crazy? So you can do that again? Forget that, buddy."

"I may be able to forget it," he said solemnly, with a hint of chastisement, "but you won't. The pain isn't going to go away. In fact, it will get worse. Much worse. You should have seen a doctor days ago."

"It's already worse—no thanks to you."

"Miss Majors."

"For heaven's sake, call me Marjorie."

"Marjorie, then. I .nning out of here like a terrified rabbit isn't going to make everything all right."

So he'd noticed the way she was eyeing the neat pile of her folded clothes. She wouldn't run, because that would be silly and stupid, but she couldn't keep from looking at the door longingly.

"You have an inflamed appendix."

She swallowed past the tightness in her throat. The shooting pain hadn't ebbed; if anything it had gotten steadily worse from the moment he had set his fingers upon her tender abdomen. Oh, dear God, her appendix. She didn't need a fortune-teller to explain what would happen next. Surgery. The sound of the word was as ominous as that of a trumpet in a funeral march.

"Your temperature is rising, and my guess is that the white cell count is sky-high," he continued. "A blood test will confirm that easily enough."

A weak smile wobbled at the corners of her mouth. "My appendix," she repeated.

Sam nodded. "Go ahead and get dressed. When you've finished, I'll have my nurse draw some blood and escort you into my office. That'll give me a few minutes to make the necessary arrangements. We'll talk, and I'll explain where we go from here."

"Okay." Her voice sounded scratchy and thin, like an ailing frog's.

He eyed her again, his gaze tender and concerned. He deeply regretted having hurt her. The look of suppressed pain in her eyes bothered him greatly, and he tried to lend her some of his own confidence. "Don't look so worried—everything's going to be fine."

"Everything's going to be fine," Marjorie echoed, unable to disguise the sarcasm. "Sure it is." The minute he vacated the room, she snapped her teeth over her bottom lip and bit down unmercifully. Her hand trembled as she brushed a thick strand of hair away from her face, and the room appeared to sway slightly. The last time she'd felt this shaky had been at her parents' funeral.

As if on cue, the nurse reappeared when Marjorie had completed dressing. She led her into another room and drew blood from her arm.

While he waited for Marjorie, Sam contacted Cal Johnson, a surgeon and good friend. His instincts told him the sooner they had her in the hospital, the better. When he explained her symptoms to Cal, his friend concurred and agreed to take the case. His second telephone conversation was with a member of the staff at Tacoma General.

Marjorie appeared in the doorway of his office, and Sam saw her from the corner of his eye. She hesitated, and he motioned for her to come inside and take a seat.

"I don't think we should wait any longer," he said into the receiver. "Good. Good. Yes, I can have her over there in a half hour. I'll assist."

In an effort to keep from looking as though she were listening in on his conversation, Marjorie's gaze scanned the walls. Certificates, diplomas and service awards decorated the surface. His desk was neat and orderly. The sure sign of a twisted mind, she mused darkly. She glanced his way again and sighed. Heavens, she hoped that he wasn't discussing her! He must have been. If he felt surgery was necessary, then she'd like a couple of days to mentally prepare herself. A week should do it.

Marjorie's soft, expressive eyes pleaded with him, but Sam's gaze just missed meeting hers, and she realized that, although he hadn't mentioned her name, he wasn't likely to be talking about another patient.

"Sorry to keep you waiting," he said, when he'd finished.

"No problem." She smiled and her fingers curved around her eelskin purse in her lap.

"I was just talking to Tacoma General."

Marjorie pointed her finger over her shoulder. "Did you know that you have a dying houseplant in your waiting room?"

"I wasn't aware of that."

"You want to cut me open, don't you?"

"We don't have a lot of options here, Marjorie. I've contacted a friend of mine. He'll be doing the actual surgery, but I'll be there, as well. Your appendix is at a dangerous stage and could burst at any time."

He said her name in a soft, caressing way that would have made another woman's knees turn to tapioca pudding. Not Marjorie's. Not now. Panic was overwhelming her, dominating her thoughts and actions.

"Where's your family?" he asked in a low, reassuring voice.

"I don't have one."

The memory of the orphaned kitten returned to Sam's mind. Cold. Lost. Frightened. And vulnerable.

At his look of surprise, Marjorie hurried to explain, "No parents, that is...one sister, but she doesn't live in Washington state. Jody's attending the University of Portland."

"What about a boyfriend?"

With effort she held her head high, her chin jutting out proudly. "I've only been in Washington a few months." She was about to add that she didn't have time to date much, not when she had to earn enough money to support herself and keep her sister in school. She managed to stop in the nick of time. This man was almost a complete stranger, and she had been about to spill her guts to him. He had that effect upon her, and Marjorie found that oddly intimidating.

"Is there anyone you can call?"

"No." No one she felt she could trouble. She'd made it on her own this far; she'd get through surgery and a lot more if necessary. "When do you want to do the surgery?"

"Soon. Cal Johnson will make that decision."

The lump worked its way up the delicate column of her neck. The battle to hold back the fear was nearly overwhelming. Even breathing normally had become a difficult task as she labored to appear unaffected and calm.

"So you won't be doing the surgery?" This was a man she could trust. Marjorie, like the others, had known that instinctively. Now he was pawning her off on another physician, and the thought was almost as terrifying as the actual operation.

"Do you think you should trust a doctor with a dying houseplant?"

"I...don't know." Marjorie realized he was attempting to help her relax, and she appreciated the effort. He really was a nice man. Lydia and the others were right about that. She envisioned him with other women, lending security and assurance. He'd chosen his profession well.

"I may not have a green thumb, but when it comes to surgery you don't have any worries."

"Then why won't you do this one?"

"The appendix isn't my área of expertise. Dr. Johnson has done countless appendectomies, whereas I've only done a few. I'll assist."

"But I know you." As soon as the words ran over her tongue, Marjorie realized how ridiculous they sounded. They'd met less than a half hour earlier.

"You'll do fine with Dr. Johnson."

"I suppose I will," she said without much confidence.

"I can honestly say that you're the first woman who's jumped off the examination table, ready to swing at me." His smiling eyes studied her.

"Hey, that poke hurt."

"I know, and I apologize," he answered sincerely. "I don't want you to worry about this surgery. I'll be there with you. Cal Johnson's an excellent surgeon, and there shouldn't be any problems since we've caught this in time."

Marjorie nodded.

"I'm not going to let you down."

"You say that to all your patients, don't you?"

"No." His eyes widened briefly. "Here." He opened the top drawer and took out a single sheet of paper. "Let me show you what we're going to do."

Marjorie wasn't sure she wanted to know. He must have read the doubt in her eyes, because he added, "I learned long ago that my patients aren't nearly as nervous if they have an idea of what's going to happen."

Marjorie nodded and cocked her head so that she could see his drawing.

"As you're probably aware, the appendix is a small pocket, from one to six inches in size. It serves no purpose." He illustrated it, dexterously moving his pencil across the sheet of paper.

Marjorie understood only a little about what he was telling her, but nodded as though she had recently graduated from medical school and knew it all.

He talked for several minutes more, explaining where Dr. Johnson would be making the incision and what he'd be doing. "Once you're admitted to the hospital, you'll undergo a series of tests, including several X rays."

"X rays? Why?"

"We want to be sure that your lungs aren't congested. No need to borrow trouble."

"I see," Marjorie commented, although she wasn't sure of any of this. Whatever he and the other doctors thought was fine with her.

"You'll only be in the hospital three or four days, depending on how you feel, and back to work within three weeks."

"Three weeks," Marjorie echoed. "I can't take off that much time!"

"You don't have any choice."

"Wanna bet?" Defiantly she slapped a challenge at him. "In case you don't realize it, a car salesperson works solely on commission. If I don't sell cars, I don't eat."

His mouth tightened momentarily. "Let's play that part by ear. No doubt you'll surprise me."

"No doubt," she echoed.

Sam rubbed the pencil between his palms. "How'd you get into car sales?"

Marjorie shrugged. "The usual way, I suppose. I started out working in a computer store four or five years back. We worked on commission and I did well."

"That figures."

"I liked the challenge, and nothing held me back from making the kind of money I wanted, except my own limitations."

"Where'd you go from there?"

"Boats."

"Do you know that much about them?"

She crossed her knees, winced in an effort to hide the pain, then grinned sheepishly. Naturally he noticed, but was kind enough not to comment. "At the time I didn't know a thing about watercraft, but before long I learned everything there was to know."

"From there it was a natural progression to cars?"

"More or less. I like selling a top-of-the-line product, so selling Mercedes sedans and sports cars was a natural step."

"I don't imagine there are many women in the car-sales business." The pencil continued working back and forth across his palms. He didn't normally spend this much time with a patient, but he wanted her to feel comfortable with him. She was alone and scared to death, and it was his job to do what he could to reassure her. Success in health care had a lot to do with attitude, and he wanted Marjorie Majors to feel confident and secure about whatever lay ahead.

"There are a few women in sales, and the number's growing."

"I've always wanted a Mercedes."

Marjorie realized he was doing everything he could to ease her fears and help her relax. It had worked, and the tense terror that had gripped her only moments before had slipped away.

He placed his hands against the edge of the desk and rolled back his chair. "I'll see you at Tacoma General," he said, his gaze holding hers.

"I wasn't planning to run away."

"I didn't honestly think you would."

The smile that bracketed his mouth did funny things to her heart rate, but Marjorie quickly dismissed the effect as having anything to do with romance. She was grateful, that was it. Grateful—nothing less, nothing more.

Chapter Two

Marjorie felt rummy. She lay on her back, staring above her as the dotted white tile loomed closer and closer, then gradually faded back into place. Her eyes narrowed, and she tried to tell herself that the ceiling wasn't actually closing in on her. This phenomenon was the result of the shot the nurse had given her a few minutes earlier to help her relax before rolling her into the operating room.

"How are you feeling?" Sam Bretton moved beside her gurney and placed his hand over hers.

Again Marjorie was struck by how gentle his dark eyes were. A man shouldn't possess sensitive eyes like that. In her drugged condition her imagination was running away with her, suggesting thoughts she had no right to think. She stared back at the good doctor, blinked twice because it seemed as though she could see straight into his heart. It was large and full, and the capacity to care and love seemed boundless.

"Marjorie?"

She pulled her gaze past the I.V. bottle to Sam and lightly shook her head in a futile effort to clear her befuddled mind. "You wouldn't believe the things they did to me," she said, trying to disregard the strange effect of the medication.

"You met Cal Johnson?"

She nodded. He wasn't another Sam Bretton, but he'd do, especially if Sam felt he would.

"So they put you through the mill?"

His smile dazzled Marjorie, and she reminded herself anew that at the moment her senses couldn't be trusted. "You must have telephoned ahead, because there was a whole crew just waiting to get their hands on me the minute I walked in the door."

"You can thank Cal for that. I'm only here to assist."

"Sure you are! If you think I believe that, then there's some swampland in Nevada that might interest me, as well, right?"

"Are you saying you don't trust me?" Sam's eyes widened with feigned outrage. He liked Marjorie. Even now, when she was dopey with medication and sleepy from the effects, he found her sense of humor stimulating. Her ready smile had wrapped itself around him the moment he'd walked into the room. She was fresh and alive; her mind was active, her wit lively and her courage, under the circumstances, admirable.

"I'll have you know that in the last hour I've been poked, pinched, prodded and a bunch of other disgusting things I don't even want to discuss."

His lips trembled with suppressed mirth, and he squeezed her fingers reassuringly. "Is there anything I can get you?"

Marjorie tried to smile, but her mouth refused to cooperate. "That sounds suspiciously like a last request."

The dark eyes that studied her crinkled at the corners as he revealed his amusement. "It wasn't."

"You mean I don't need to ask for a priest?"

"Not this time around. Anything else?"

The inside of her mouth felt thick and dry. "Something to drink. Please."

He reached behind him and took a chip of ice from the water jug. Again the urge to reassure her, to stay with her was strong. Her hair spilled out across the pillow, and the red highlights suggested that her temper would be as quick as her smile. "This will have to do for now. Suck on it and make it last."

Obediently she opened her mouth, and he slipped the dripping ice inside and paused to wipe a drop of moisture from her chin. It wasn't until then that Marjorie noticed he was dressed entirely in green. A cap covered his head, and a surgical mask hung free around his neck.

"Green surgical gowns?" she asked, holding the ice chip against the back side of her mouth so she could speak clearly. "Is that because red stains are so difficult to remove from white fabric?" She sucked in her breath and closed her eyes. "Don't answer that—I don't want to know."

"Don't let your guard down now, Marjorie, you're doing fine."

Her eyes shot open. "It's not you who's going under the knife, fellow. I'll be scared if I want, and I don't mind telling you, I'd rather be anyplace else in the world but right here." Shot or no shot, relaxant or no relaxant, she'd never been more unsure about anything. To this point in her healthful existence, a painful ear infection had been her only medical ailment. Now that she thought about it, Marjorie was astonished that she had admitted how afraid she was to Sam. It wasn't like her. That shot must have contained a truth serum.

"Everything's going to work out," he said in that calm, confident voice of his.

Without much effort Marjorie could envision him talking someone out of jumping off the Tacoma Narrows Bridge. He had the kind of voice a salesman would kill for—low-pitched, confident, effortless, sincere.

"Don't worry," she said with feigned composure, seeing herself standing on the edge of the steel precipice, looking into the swirling waters far below. "I'm not going to jump."

He gave her a funny look but made no comment.

"That didn't make any sense, did it?" Marjorie tossed her head from side to side in an effort to clear her thoughts. It didn't work. Everything scrambled together until she wasn't sure of anything.

His hand patted hers. "Don't worry about it. The medication has that effect."

Marjorie wondered if it actually was the shot. No, she was convinced his silk-edged voice and kind eyes were the cause of all this, mesmerizing her. Her eyes drifted closed, and she moistened her lips as she imagined Sam Bretton leaning over her and whispering words of love in her ear, then taking her in his arms and kissing her with such tenderness, such passion that her thoughts forcefully collided inside her head. A fireworks display that rivaled the Fourth-of-July celebration exploded, and she forced her eyes open and felt the blood rush through her veins.

"Go ahead and sleep," he said softly. "I'll be here when you wake up."

"Please don't leave me." Her eyes rounded, and her mouth filled with the bitter taste of panic. She needed this stranger, this man she barely knew, more than she'd ever needed anyone. The terror that gripped her as she stared ahead at the wide double doors that led to the operating room was intense and nearly overwhelming.

"I'm not going anywhere," Sam assured her, continuing to hold her hand, his fingers firmly entwined with hers.

Somehow it seemed vitally important that he be there every minute. Still, she hated to need anyone. People had always let her down. She was a stronger person than this, and Dr. Sam Bretton was little more than a stranger. Yet she trusted him enough to place her life in his capable hands.

"Don't worry, I'll be fine," she said, and realized her voice was barely audible. "You...you don't need to stay with me. I'm a big girl. I'll get through this...really...don't tell Jody, she'll only worry...must call Lydia."

"That's all taken care of," he said, and his voice seemed to come from a great distance.

"Thank you, Sam," Marjorie mumbled, and slipped into a light sleep.

"Dr. Johnson is ready, doctor."

An invisible force pushed the gurney forward, and Marjorie struggled to open her eyes. Someone lifted her head and placed her hair inside a confining cap.

Unable to resist, Marjorie opened one eye and was greeted by blinding lights. Sam was at her side, and Cal Johnson stood on the opposite side of the room, examining her X rays. Sam leaned over her and explained that the anesthesiologist would be there any minute. Marjorie nodded, even managed a weak smile, then decided that it was better not to look around. She settled back down and tightly shut her eyes.

Soon other voices met over her head, some deep, others crisp and a few soft. In her drug-induced drowsiness Marjorie sorted through each one and tried only to assimilate Sam's words. The nurses joked and flirted with him like a longtime friend. Marjorie sighed with the fleeting knowledge that if his patients fell in love with him, then the women on the hospital staff must be equally vulnerable to his charms. Maybe he was already married. Of course, that was it! Sam

Bretton had a wife. Her disappointment was keen. He was married. He had to be. Damn! Damn! Damn! All the good ones were already taken!

It got too difficult to concentrate, and she soon gave up trying. When she woke, this troublesome episode would all be over, and she could get on with her life and forget that any of this had ever happened.

Impatiently Marjorie waded through huge billows of thick, black fog. She shivered with cold and sighed when Sam's familiar voice asked for a heated blanket. She felt the weight of a quilt on top of her, and she sighed contentedly. The fog parted as warmth seeped into her bones, and for the first time she could decipher a path that led through the haze. She tried to speak, but her lips seemed glued together, and no amount of effort could pry them apart.

"Marjorie?"

Getting her eyes to open required an equal amount of strain, but when she managed that task, she was blinded by a flash of high-density light. She groaned and lowered her lashes.

"Am I in the morgue?" she mumbled, having difficulty getting all the words over her uncooperative tongue.

"Not yet," Sam answered.

"That's reassuring."

"You're in the recovery room. Everything went without a hitch. We're lucky we got the appendix when we did. From the look of it the whole thing was ready to burst, and then there could have been some unpleasant complications."

"Close, but no cigar."

"In this case you don't want a cigar."

"So I'll live and love again?"

Sam brushed the hair from her temple. "You're good for at least another fifty years."

For some inexplicable reason it seemed easier to speak with her eyes closed. Her lids fluttered shut even though she strained to keep them open a moment longer.

"Go ahead and sleep," Sam told her softly. "I'm here, like I promised."

Marjorie wanted to thank him; she searched for some way to let him know how grateful she was that she hadn't woken up alone. The hospital may seem a warm, congenial place to him, but he was there every day. To Marjorie it was a disinfected torture chamber, and she was scared witless. It seemed so important to tell him that his presence comforted her that she wrestled to keep awake even as she felt herself slipping back into the thick, dark fog.

Pain woke Marjorie up the second time—a dull, throbbing ache in her side. It was quite different from what she'd experienced before meeting Sam. She raised her hand, rubbed her eyes and yawned. She room wasn't as brilliant as before. The light appeared muted and she was grateful. She rolled her head and realized she was in a small room. The drapes were closed, but a ribbon of light permeated the small enclosure. A noise, a movement ever so feeble, distracted her, and she turned her head in the opposite direction and discovered Sam Bretton sitting at her bedside reading the latest novel of Mary Higgins Clark.

"Sam?"

He closed the book, turned to face her and smiled. "Hello again."

"What time is it?"

He rotated his wrist. "Almost six."

"In the morning?"

Sam nodded and stood, setting his novel aside. He took her limp wrist and pressed his fingers over her pulse while he stared at the face of his watch.

"Have you been here all night?" It seemed incredible that he would have stayed with her all through the night. She noticed then that the blood-pressure cuff was wrapped around her upper arm, and fear renewed itself within her. There'd been problems! Big problems! She swallowed around the tightness in her throat. All night she'd teetered on the brink of death, and Sam had stayed with her and fought for her very life. For hours her fate had hung upon a delicate balance, and one man had valiantly battled to save her.

"What happened?" Her question was hoarse, revealing a hundred doubts.

"Nothing," he answered crisply. "All surgeries should be such a breeze."

"Nothing went wrong?"

He frowned, puzzled. "Nothing."

"But you stayed with me all night. Why?"

The frown thickened, marring his smooth brow with three nearly straight lines. "Because I said I would. You needed someone."

Guilt fell heavily upon her shoulders. She certainly hadn't meant for him to do this. He must have gone without sleep the entire night and all because of a few silly words she'd uttered in the throes of panic. "But, I didn't . . ."

"Hey, don't worry about me," he interrupted quickly. "I've got the day off."

"I suppose you golf on Wednesdays?" she asked.

"I don't play golf."

Marjorie feigned shock. "You don't golf? Just what kind of doctor are you? No one told me that before I made my first appointment with you."

"Count your blessings, Majors."

"Oh?"

"I could charge by the hour."

The effort to smile was painful, but holding back her amusement would have been impossible. "Hey, don't make me laugh—it hurts." She groaned and placed her hand over her abdomen. "Why does it hurt now? I thought the pain would go away."

"It will in a few days."

"A whole lot of good that's doing me now."

"Stop being so impatient, Marjorie."

He said her name with just enough of a challenge for her to quit arguing. She would grin and bear it.

"I'll get the nurse," Sam informed her, grinning. "Cal left instructions for you to sit upright once you woke."

Marjorie snapped her mouth closed and pressed her lips together to smother a protest. Dr. Johnson didn't actually expect her to move her body! She couldn't—not yet. If breathing hurt this much, she could well imagine the agony that sitting up would cause. Great! Sam and his friend had grabbed her from the jaws of death only to let her die a slow, torturous death from pain.

From the moment she'd met Dr. Sam, Marjorie had been looking for some imperfection. Anything. He was much too wonderful to be real. Now the flaw stood out like a fake diamond under a jeweler's eyepiece. Sam Bretton enjoyed watching people suffer.

Again Sam proved her wrong. The nurse who came to her room came alone. Her name tag was pinned to her uniform—Bertha Powell, R.N.

"Dr. Sam sent me," Bertha announced.

Marjorie studied the older woman, who looked as though her previous profession had been mud wrestling. She was built as solid as a rock, and from the glinting light in her eyes, she was just waiting for Marjorie to start something.

"Where's Sam?"

"*Doctor* Sam asked me to tell you that he'll be back later this afternoon."

"Wonderful," Marjorie muttered, and wiggled her big toe as an experiment. The pain wasn't debilitating, but she wasn't exactly up to swinging from grapevines, either.

Bertha pulled back the sheet. "Are you ready?"

Marjorie wondered what the other woman would do if she announced that she refused to move. Briefly she toyed with the idea, then decided against it. Her teeth gritted, she cautiously did what had been requested of her.

Exhausted afterward, Marjorie slept for six hours. Someone moving inside her room woke her. When she stirred and opened her eyes, she found Lydia standing at the foot of her bed with a small bouquet of flowers in her hand.

"Hi, Marjorie," Lydia said in a soft singsong voice.

"I had my appendix out," Marjorie grumbled. "I stopped your friend in the nick of time from doing a lobotomy."

Lydia looked relieved and set the flowers on the bedside table. "Same ol' Marjorie."

"I didn't mean to snap at you."

"Hey, no problem. I'm used to it, remember?"

Marjorie tried to wipe the tiredness from her eyes. "I bet you're waiting for me to tell you how right you were."

"It'd feel good, but I can wait." Obviously she couldn't, because she added, "Didn't I tell you it had to be more than a queasy stomach? I was the one who figured it out long before you, wasn't I?"

"By golly you did," Marjorie returned, with more than a hint of amused sarcasm. "Where would I be without you?" That much wasn't in jest. She was sincerely grateful her friend had made the appointment when she did, especially after what Sam had told her.

Lydia pulled a chair close to the hospital bed and plunked herself down. Without so much as pausing to inhale, she started off with another long series of questions. "How do you like Dr. Sam? Isn't he wonderful? Didn't I tell you he was a marvel? Now that you've met him, you'll probably be like everyone else and fall madly in love with him."

"No doubt."

Lydia's face blossomed into a wide grin. "I knew you'd like him."

Just managing to avoid her friend's gaze, Marjorie asked, "What's his wife like?"

"His wife?" That stopped Lydia cold. She opened and closed her mouth twice. "I didn't know he was married."

"You mean he isn't?" Hope flared eternal. Naw, he had to be married—and probably had a passel of kids to boot. All in diapers, no doubt. Knowing the type of doctor he was convinced Marjorie that Sam Bretton would be a devoted husband and father. She, on the other hand, was definitely not the mother type.

"I don't know anything about his wife," Lydia answered thoughtfully, chewing on the corner of her bottom lip. "I don't think he's married. I can't remember seeing a wedding band, can you?"

"It doesn't matter," Marjorie muttered. He'd been wonderful ... more than wonderful, but she had far more important matters to deal with that didn't involve risking her heart over a physician whose moonlighting job entailed tossing women's equilibriums off balance.

In order to change the subject Marjorie scooted her gaze past Lydia to the bouquet of carnations and roses on the bedside table. "Thanks for the flowers."

"Hey, no problem. They're from all the salesmen at Dixon's."

"All?" Marjorie cocked one delicately shaped brow suspiciously. "Even Al Swanson?"

Lydia grinned sheepishly. "He tossed in a buck and suggested I buy a cactus."

That Marjorie could believe. Al obviously didn't approve of women in the car business. That was tough, she mused, since she was at Dixon Motors for the long haul no matter what Al or anyone else thought. It wasn't that Al had taken a dislike to her and her alone. Al had a problem with everyone. He had yet to learn that sales work was often a team effort. Marjorie's gut feeling was that Al Swanson wouldn't be around Dixon much longer.

"Oh!" Lydia exclaimed. "I nearly forgot. Dr. Sam phoned and told me to get the key to your apartment so I could pick up some personal items you're going to need."

Once again the good physician had amazed Marjorie with his thoughtfulness. "I hate to put you to all the trouble."

"It's no trouble. Honest. You'd do the same thing for me."

Marjorie smiled her thanks. Accepting another's assistance was so difficult for her—more than it should have been, she realized. She'd practically raised Jody with little or no help from state agencies. With a limited college education she'd forged her own way in the world, designed her career and earned enough to support herself and pay for her sister's college tuition. Sam Bretton had the wrong impression of her, and to Marjorie's utter embarrassment, she had to admit she'd been the one to give it to him.

"The key," Lydia reminded her.

"Oh, it's in my purse." Guessing where it would be stored, she nodded toward the closet door.

Lydia stood and moved in that direction. "Dr. Sam gave me a list, but you might want to read it over."

"I'm sure he thought of everything," Marjorie responded distractedly. She had to set Sam straight. She wasn't a helpless clinging vine, although he had good reason to believe so. The memory of how she'd pleaded with him not to leave her was a keen source of her present chagrin.

Triumphantly Lydia held up Marjorie's key chain. "I'll run over to your place and get your things now."

Marjorie could do little more than nod. Her thoughts were light-years ahead of her, spinning out of control. She'd talk to Sam the next time he stopped in to see her. She'd explain everything. Yawning, she placed her hand over her mouth and determinedly tried to suppress the exhaustion that gripped her. How strange it felt to become so weary so easily. Of their own accord, her eyes drifted closed.

Sam was there when she woke. He smiled down on her before noting something on her chart. "How's the patient feeling?"

"I don't know yet, give me a minute to sort through the various pains." To her surprise Marjorie noticed that her purple velvet housecoat was neatly folded across the bottom of her bed. Lydia must have returned with her things, and Marjorie had somehow managed to sleep through her friend's second visit.

"Dr. Johnson wants you up and walking before dinner."

The protest that sprang automatically to her lips died a quick death. Sitting on the edge of the bed had been difficult enough! Sam had to be out of his mind if he believed she was going to traipse around this room or down these halls, dragging an I.V. bottle with her, and all because some man she barely knew had ordered such. She, of all people, should know when she was ready to risk life and limb by walking again.

Sam glanced up from his notations, his eyes studying her. "What, no argument?"

"When can I get out of here?"

"Soon, but that's up to Cal," he answered noncommittally. "Listen, before you think about leaving the hospital, focus your energy on getting out of bed and moving."

He sounded so reasonable, so calm and confident that the brick walls of her rebellion crumbled before she had them completely raised. With the aid of her feet, Marjorie cautiously moved aside the sheet and struggled into a sitting position.

"Marjorie, for God's sake, don't try to move on your own." Sam closed the metal chart with a loud click and shoved it aside.

"No," she said through gritted teeth. "I'll do it myself." One foot freed itself from the tangled sheet, and she raised herself up onto one elbow.

Disregarding her words, Sam placed his arm around her shoulders and helped her into an upright position. Flushed and embarrassed by how incredibly weak she was, Marjorie reached for her housecoat, astonished that the simple task of sitting could tire her so much that she was practically panting.

Sam located her slippers for her and slipped them onto her feet. "Okay, let's take this nice and easy."

"I'm not exactly ready to jump off this bed and race down the corridor." The spinning room gradually circled into place and came to a stop. "I think I'd feel better about this in the morning."

"Now, Marjorie."

She wanted to argue with him, but hadn't the strength. "I'm not normally like this," she said, with as much force as she could muster. "I'm sorry I asked you to stay with me.... I realize now I shouldn't have...."

"Marjorie, I stayed because I wanted to, not out of any obligation." He stepped around the bed and stood directly in front of her. Because the hospital bed was so high off the floor, their eyes met. His were warm and sincere, while hers flashed with frustration and regret.

Although his words filled her with an absurd amount of pleasure, Marjorie still felt compelled to explain herself. "But I'm not like that . . . really."

"Like what?"

"Weak and sniveling."

"I never once thought that."

"Oh, you're impossible!"

Sam's thick brows shot upward. "I'm what?"

Marjorie lightly tossed her head to and fro. "Nothing."

"Do you doubt my word?"

"Not exactly. It's just that I feel I've given you the wrong impression of me. I'm a capable, responsible adult. Good grief, I even figured out my own taxes last year."

"I'm impressed." He pushed a small stool across the floor so she could use that as a step to climb off the bed.

"You're actually going to make me do this?" Marjorie couldn't seem to get her body to cooperate. One foot eased itself downward as she cautiously scooted to the edge of the mattress.

Sam placed a supporting arm under her elbow to help her down. She felt small and incredibly fragile in his embrace. Once again she reminded him of the rain-drenched kitten he'd discovered all those years ago. And like the half-drowned feline, Marjorie Majors required love and attention, too. Only Sam wasn't in any position to give it to her. She was his patient, not a love interest. The two didn't mix. Couldn't mix.

Both feet were firmly planted on the floor and Marjorie paused, half expecting to keel over. When she didn't, she felt a glowing sense of triumph. She'd made it, actually made it.

"Good girl," Sam said, and reluctantly dropped his arm. "Now take a few steps."

"You don't mean for me to walk, do you?" She was only hours from having been under the knife, hours from knocking on death's door. Hours from the most frightening experience of her life.

"I want you to walk. Walk. You know, one foot in front of the other in a forward motion."

She flashed him a look of irritation.

"And later, if you're a good girl, I'll take you upstairs."

"Upstairs? Is there something up there that would interest me? Like food?"

"You're hungry?"

"Famished! I haven't eaten in two days." That was entirely true. Marjorie liked her food and seldom skipped a meal. Luckily, gaining weight had never been a problem. She guessed she was fortunate in that department, but she would quickly melt away if this hospital had anything to do with it.

The liquid diet wasn't going to please her, Sam knew, but her digestive system couldn't handle anything more for a few days. He decided against telling her as much. He'd leave as many unpleasant tasks as possible for Cal Johnson. After all, Cal was the physician of record.

While guiding the I.V. pole beside her, Sam manipulated them out the wide doorway and into the broad hallway.

"This afternoon while you were sleeping, I delivered a set of identical twins," Sam boasted proudly.

Birth, even after countless deliveries, had never ceased to humble him. Twins were always special. "They're upstairs," he continued. "I'll take you to see them later, if you want."

Marjorie looked at him and blinked. She didn't know how to explain that babies frightened her. All right, they terrorized her. Some women took to motherhood and dirty diapers like hogs to mud. But, unfortunately, such would never be the case with Marjorie. The only time she'd ever been around babies, they cried. Within ten minutes she was ready to wail herself. After several embarrassing episodes in her youth, Marjorie had decided that anyone under two was allergic to her.

"I . . . I think I'd better wait until I've got more strength," she said, straining her voice.

"Of course," Sam agreed. "I wouldn't dream of dragging you upstairs your first time out. Tomorrow maybe, or the next day."

"Sure. Anytime," Marjorie answered, but the words nearly stuck in her throat.

Chapter Three

Marjorie stared at the orange tray and grimaced in pure disgust. If she so much as looked at another bowl of plain gelatin, she was going to start screaming and say something unladylike that would shock the entire hospital staff. It appeared that no one in all of Tacoma General believed in honest-to-goodness home-cooked meals. What they'd brought in to her the past two days only vaguely resembled food.

"Good morning," the nurse's aid greeted, as she strolled into the room. "And how was your breakfast?"

"You don't want to know."

The young girl glanced at the untouched tray. "You didn't eat a thing."

"I couldn't," Marjorie muttered disparagingly. It wasn't the poor girl's fault that the hospital had chosen to starve her.

"Aren't you feeling better? Usually my patients are more than ready to eat by this time. Are you in a lot of pain? Perhaps I should notify Dr. Johnson."

"Contacting the doctor isn't going to convince me to eat...this. I'd rather die," Marjorie admitted dramatically. "I refuse to swallow anything that slithers down the back of my throat."

The girl chuckled. "Let me see what I can do." She left and Marjorie stared after her longingly. Visions of cheesy pizza, crisp fried chicken and a thick, juicy steak played havoc with her imagination. Marjorie was convinced she smelled bacon frying in the distance, the odor wafting toward her and swirling around her head, tormenting her with delicious dreams.

"Problems?" Sam sauntered into the room, looking sympathetic.

"Sam," Marjorie said, and brightened instantly. She hadn't seen him in nearly twenty hours and had rarely been more pleased to lay eyes on anyone. Sam Bretton could be trusted. She wasn't so sure about anyone else in this antiseptic place, but Sam would help straighten out this unfortunate mess.

"You didn't eat your breakfast." His voice was only lightly accusing.

"I couldn't," she said, her eyes softly pleading with his. "The mush had more lumps than a camel, and only God knows what flavor of Jell-O they wanted me to eat.... Liver, I think, and even with a whipped topping, it looked disgusting.''

"The tea and dry toast?"

"Oh, they were fine, I suppose, but I didn't touch either one—it was the principle of the thing. Why can't I have a mushroom omelet with toast and jelly on the side? Something... anything, but gelatin and mush."

"Soon."

Marjorie's face mirrored her reaction. Obviously *soon* wasn't going to be this morning, and she needed nourishment *now*, if not earlier. Disappointment consumed her. She'd thought of Sam as her ally, her friend. The amazing part was that he seemed to look better to her every time he walked in the room. The fog had cleared from the first day or two that followed the surgery, and the one vivid memory was of Sam. When he was with her, even the pain lessened. He filled her room with an assurance of well-being and safekeeping. He lent her confidence, stamina and the conviction that this, too, would pass, and when it did, he'd be there for her.

Sam's hand reached for hers, and his eyes gentled in a kind, tender way.

"Marjorie, listen." He did understand her position, but she had to realize that food had to be reintroduced gradually into her digestive system. "You're not being a good patient."

"Oh, spare me," she snapped, quickly losing a grip on her fragile patience. Her temper was always quick to fire when she was overly hungry. "No one told me I had to pretend I was on the good ship Lollipop."

"All we're asking is that you do as we say."

"And die of starvation in the process."

"Don't be so dramatic. You're a long way from that. Most women look forward to dropping a few pounds during their hospital stay." The moment the words slipped from Sam's mouth, he recognized what a terrible mistake he'd made. It was too late to retract his statement; his only hope was that she'd let it slide. He tried smiling, praying the action would take any sting from his words. It didn't.

Marjorie's face grew as red as a California pepper, and her anger was just as hot. "Are you insinuating Tacoma General is a fat farm and that I'm overweight?"

"No, you misunderstood..."

"Your meaning was more than clear," she said coldly, and reached for the buzzer that rang for the nurse. Immediately the red light above her bed flashed on.

"Marjorie...I didn't mean to be so tactless. You're not the least bit plump.... I'm doing a poor job of this." Sam wiped a hand around the back of his neck and sighed. He regretted getting trapped in this no-win conversation. Usually when it came to dealing with his patients, he had more finesse than this.

She ignored him and tossed aside the sheet, sticking her bare leg out in an ungraceful effort to climb down from the high hospital bed. "Nurse," she cried, but her voice was weak and wobbly.

"Marjorie, I must insist you stay where you are and eat your breakfast."

Their eyes met and clashed. Marjorie was hurting and hungry, a lethal combination that resulted in the most embarrassing reaction. Tears. Then, when she tried to speak, her voice was a full octave higher and in danger of shattering the nearby window. Swallowing her shame, Marjorie proudly turned her face away from him and motioned toward the door, wordlessly asking him to leave.

Sam hesitated. Once again his heart went out to her, and he had to force himself to walk out of the room. In the few days since he'd met Marjorie, she'd touched him in ways few women ever had. He had been a silent witness to her courage and realized that she possessed a rare personal strength. Her laughter was a sweet melody to his ears, her movements dominated by an inherent gracefulness. Several times over the past twenty-four hours, he'd found his thoughts drifting to her, and he smiled at the memory of her waking from the operation to ask if she was in the morgue. At each meeting he realized all the more how damnably proud she was. Proud. Fiery. Straightforward. He found it utterly astonishing that she wasn't married. And he was grateful. He'd like to get to know her better—a whole lot better.

Sam knew he'd made a mess of this and was angry with himself. He patted her shoulder and turned to leave the room.

The nurse's aid met him outside her door and raised questioning eyes to him. "Doctor?"

"I believe she'll eat her breakfast now," Sam answered, his thoughts distracted.

"Very good." The younger woman beamed him a warm smile, no doubt impressed with his ability to deal with a difficult situation.

Sam did his best to return the friendly gesture. He had a reputation for working well with unreasonable patients. Marjorie wasn't that, only confused and miserable.

And he'd made a mess of things.

Marjorie heard Sam tell the nurse's aid that she'd be eating her meal and glared after him, half tempted to toss the liver Jell-O at his arrogant backside. She didn't, though, because he was right. Once again she'd made an idiot of herself in front of him and half the hospital staff. She didn't like herself when she behaved this way and yet seemed powerless to change.

The moisture on her cheek felt like burning acid, and she brushed the tears aside, thoroughly embarrassed by their appearance. She wasn't a crybaby, at least she hadn't been until Sam Bretton walked into her life. Then everything had quickly fallen to pieces. Whatever it was about that insufferable, wonderful man that reduced her to this state should be outlawed!

The tea was only lukewarm, but strong enough to satisfy Marjorie's need for caffeine. The dry wheat toast was surprisingly filling, and the mush passable as long as she dumped three sugar packets over the top. The gelatin she ignored.

In order to avoid the gloating, triumphant look of the nurse's aid, Marjorie pretended to be asleep when the girl returned for the tray. To her surprise she did fall into a restful sleep and woke midmorning with a television game show blaring from the set positioned against the wall.

"I see you're awake." The mud-wrestling star was back. Bertha Powell, R.N., looked stiff in her starched white uniform. "Dr. Johnson wants you up and walking today. Ten laps."

"Laps?" Marjorie repeated, still caught in the last dregs of sleep. The hospital obviously provided a racecourse for surgery patients.

"The corridor," the muscular woman informed her primly. "Ten times up and back. That's your goal for today. But don't do too much at once. Two or three round trips at a time. No more."

Marjorie resisted the urge to salute. Bertha Powell seemed to be looking for a few good men—or women—to gleefully whip into shape. Marjorie didn't doubt that the woman would count every single lap.

To her credit the nurse aided Marjorie into an upright position and helped her on with her robe. There was some confusion with the tube from the I.V. bottle, but Bertha figured it out within seconds, and Marjorie's course was set. After only a few minutes she was on her way.

Steadier on her feet than before, Marjorie was pleased with her slow but sure progress. Although it was hours until noon, the hospital was a hive of activity. If she'd been in a grumbling mood, Marjorie would have pointed out that Dr. Johnson had suggested she get plenty of rest, but the hospital staff had awakened her before the sun was anywhere close to the horizon. The only people up at that time of the morning were mass murderers, teenagers and nurse's aids.

The girl who had brought in her breakfast tray grinned as Marjorie passed the nurses' station.

"Hey, you're doing great."

Marjorie smiled back. "Yes, I think I'll donate my body to science."

"Science fiction might appreciate it more" came the deep male voice from behind her.

"Sam?" Marjorie laughed and twisted her head around, pleased to see him again.

"To your room, young lady," he instructed.

Marjorie was more than happy to comply and glanced with wide-eyed curiosity toward the brown paper sack in his hand. "What's that?"

"You'll see."

He closed the door once she was safely inside the room.

"I thought you had appointments all day," she exclaimed, not that she was disappointed to see him. Nothing could have been farther from the truth; she was overjoyed.

"I just finished my rounds."

"Oh." Once again Marjorie couldn't take her eyes from his dazzling smile. "How are the twins?"

"As cute as a bug's ear. I'll take you to see them this evening, if you wish."

It was all Marjorie could do to nod. She'd brought up the subject of the babies because she knew they were close to Sam's heart. She was interested, but not to the point of overcoming her instinctive apprehension. He didn't understand that bringing her anywhere near those two could be detrimental to their well-being. When the time came, she'd look through the glass and ooh and aah with appropriate enthusiasm, and Sam would never guess she was frightened to death.

"I brought you something to tide you over until lunch," Sam said, holding out the sack to her.

Marjorie took it and eagerly peeked inside. The chocolate-coated ice-cream bar produced a small squeal of delight. If they'd been anyplace else but in the middle of a hospital, she would have thrown her arms around his neck and smudged his face with kisses to thank him properly.

"Thank you, Sam. Really."

"It was a pleasure."

Those teddy-bear eyes of his seemed to look straight into her heart. "I felt terrible about the scene I made earlier," Marjorie admitted, centering her greedy gaze on the melting Dove Bar. Her mouth started to water. This man was special. Really special.

"There's no need to apologize," Sam said. "I wasn't the least bit helpful."

"But you tried to be." She didn't understand why he was so good to her, but she wasn't willing to question it. From the moment she'd walked into his office, he'd befriended her and seen her through the most difficult days of her life. All the while he had hardly left her side. No wonder his patients were so willing to admit they fell in love with him.

Sam's heart throbbed painfully with an emotion akin to desire. Marjorie's wide eyes regarded him with such sweet gratitude that it seemed the most natural thing in the world to lean forward and press his mouth to hers. He didn't, of course, but that didn't stop his imagination from running rampant. He could all but taste her honey-sweet lips. He could all but feel her mouth shaping and fitting to his own and her ripe body pressing against him.

Inhaling deeply to discipline his thoughts, Sam took a step in retreat. Marjorie Majors had caught him completely off guard. Over the years he'd been subjected to every female ploy imaginable, but the majority of women who were interested in him were mostly concerned with the money he was making and the social position that could be obtained by becoming his wife. They hadn't soured him on marriage but had made him extra cautious. He didn't succumb easily to a woman's charms, and wouldn't. He was looking for a special woman to fill a role in his life. A helpmate, a partner, a friend.

And now there was Marjorie. Her candor had caught him unaware. She was a natural beauty. Even without makeup and with her dark hair tied lifelessly away from her face, she allured him. From the moment she'd angrily jumped off his examining table, Sam had been enraptured with her temper and wit. Her very breath acted as a powerful aphrodisiac, but nothing could come of this attraction until after she was released from the hospital. Not one damn thing.

Sam left abruptly, but Marjorie was too busy eating her ice-cream bar to pay much attention. She sucked on the wooden stick, until the last bit of chocolate had long since melted on her tongue, then carefully set the stick aside as a memento of her hospital stay.

Dragging the I.V. bottle with her, she ambled down the corridor until she reached the nurses' station. There wasn't any way to be tactful about what she needed to know, but she was in dangerous territory here, feeling the way she did about Sam Bretton.

"Ms. Powell?" she said as sweetly as she could.

"Yes?" Bertha Powell glanced up from the chart she was writing on, and her wide brow narrowed with displeasure.

"I've done five laps."

"That makes five more this afternoon."

"Right."

The woman lowered her head.

"Ms. Powell?"

"Yes." Once again the older woman's voice revealed her lack of patience. She gripped the pen with both hands and glanced up at Marjorie before slowly exhaling one long breath.

"Dr. Bretton was in earlier. I was wondering if I could ask about..."

"His wife?" the older woman finished for her.

The room swayed, and the floor buckled under Marjorie's unsteady feet. She gripped the edge of the counter until she regained her sensitive balance and the hospital had righted itself once more.

"That is what you wanted to know, isn't it?" the woman pressed.

It was all Marjorie could do to respond with a movement of her head. "He's married, then?"

"Not as far as I know," Bertha announced almost kindly. "But I swear that man breaks more hearts than a teenage idol. There isn't a woman on this floor who wouldn't give her eyeteeth to be married to that man. He's the type we're all looking for."

"But..."

"Be smart, Ms. Majors and listen to the voice of experience—learn from it. All Dr. Sam's patients fall in love with him. It's gratitude, I suppose. God knows he's hunk enough to melt anyone's heart—even mine."

Marjorie clenched her jaw to hide her reaction.

"Now I don't want you to feel bad about this. It's common enough, believe me."

The heat that exploded into Marjorie's cheeks was hot enough to fry eggs. She hadn't realized her feelings were so obvious. Under normal conditions she didn't fluster easily, but when it came to Sam, she lost all her poise and aplomb.

"He's a wonderful person," Marjorie managed to say with some semblance of control.

"Honey, you don't know the half of it. I saw that man sit for hours with a young couple after their baby died. More than once I've been a witness to his tenderness—that's why I'm telling you what I am. Believe me, if I were twenty years younger, I'd be in love with the man myself. Hell, I *am* in love with him. We all are."

"Thank you." Already Marjorie was walking away, trying to disguise her embarrassment. She'd tried to be tactful, tried to find out what she could without making a total idiot of herself. And she'd failed.

Given a few moments to think the nurse's words over, Marjorie relaxed. An odd reassurance replaced her chagrin. It was good to know she was merely one of the masses. Bertha Powell was right. Women tended to fall in love with their doctors. It was a common enough malady and one she should have anticipated.

The sooner she was released from the hospital, the better, Marjorie decided. With a determination that drove her to the brink of exhaustion, she walked up and down the long corridor and fell into a deep sleep the minute the dinner tray was removed from her room.

"Morning, doctor," Marjorie answered casually, when Cal Johnson paid his morning visit. He was a bald, grandfatherly type who hadn't impressed her one way or the other.

"I see you've made considerable progress," he said, reading over her chart.

"I hope so."

"You're walking?"

"Every minute I can."

"Good." He nodded approvingly.

"When can I go home?" The question had been on her mind from the moment she talked to Bertha Powell. "I feel great—I want to go home."

"I'm pleased to hear that. However..."

"Doctor, please, I need to get home."

The grandfatherly brows molded into a tight frown. "A couple of days—maybe."

"Two days!" Marjorie would never last that long. For the sake of her sanity she had to get out of this place. Heaven only knew what would happen when she saw Sam next. The way matters were progressing, she would profess her love for him the moment he walked in the door. That was just the kind of crazy, foolish thing she'd do.

"We'll see how things progress today," Dr. Johnson claimed on his way out the door.

Marjorie wasn't given much reason to hope for an early release, and the knowledge greatly depressed her. Once again, tears hovered just beneath her eyelids.

A half hour after Dr. Johnson had left her room, Sam appeared.

"How are you feeling today?"

"Fine," Marjorie responded in a flat, emotionless tone. She did her utmost to pretend she was looking straight at him when in reality her gaze rested on the wall behind him. Even looking in Sam Bretton's direction was a dangerous pastime. She should be reassured that she was like every one of his other patients, but she wasn't. Such strong emotions were strangers to her and best avoided.

"Marjorie, what's wrong?"

"I want out of here!"

"You aren't alone, you know. Everyone who ever visits the hospital is eager to get home."

"But I feel terrific." That wasn't entirely true. "I'm as strong as an ox."

"Why don't you leave it in Dr. Johnson's hands?" he offered gently. "He knows what he's doing."

"But two days is an eternity," Marjorie insisted.

Sam's cajoling smile vanished. "Cal suggested you could leave then?"

"Yes."

"I'm sure he's mistaken."

"What do you mean?" Marjorie grumbled.

"Dr. Johnson's obviously forgotten that there isn't anyone at your apartment to watch over you when you're released."

"In case you hadn't noticed—I'm a big girl. I've been taking care of myself for a long time now. I'm not going to keel over because someone isn't there to hold my hand and place wet washcloths over my forehead every ten minutes."

"That's not the issue, Marjorie."

"Then what exactly is?"

"You've gone through a serious, life-threatening episode. Take advantage of this time to be waited on and pampered."

"Take advantage of it!" She laughed sharply. "You've got to be kidding. What's with you doctors? Do you get a kickback for every additional day a patient stays in the hospital?"

Marjorie's ability to attract him paled beside her capacity to anger him. Seldom had any words evoked such ire.

He knotted his hands into tight fists to keep from saying something he'd regret. He wasn't used to anyone arguing with him, and to suggest anything so outrageous greatly offended him.

"I think it would be best if I left."

"By all means go, Doctor."

Sam retreated, shoving the door with such rage that it nearly slammed against the wall. A kickback? Dear God, she couldn't actually believe that.

Marjorie watched him go and swallowed down a mouthful of remorse, nearly choking on the aftertaste. She hadn't meant to suggest those things, hadn't wanted to say them. But she was desperate to escape. How ironic it was that a man—a doctor who had dedicated his life to saving lives—could be responsible for breaking so many hearts.

All Marjorie wanted to do was to put this unfortunate episode behind her and get on with her life. Every day she spent in the hospital was another day without income. She hadn't been joking when she told Sam that if she didn't sell cars, she didn't eat. Most of her customers tended to glamorize her job, but it wasn't anything like they imagined. She was in a cutthroat business.

Marjorie walked the halls until she was convinced her feet had made imprints in the polished linoleum squares.

When Lydia arrived at five-thirty, Marjorie was so pleased to see her friend that she nearly tossed her arms around the other woman and wept for joy.

"How are you feeling?" Even before Marjorie had the chance to answer, Lydia continued. "You look great. I don't believe it! Your color's almost back." She slid the lone chair beside Marjorie's bed and took a seat. "Dixon's doesn't seem the same without you."

Despite her bad mood, Marjorie laughed, then sucked in a pain-wrought breath and pressed her hand against her side. She hadn't healed as much as she thought.

"Are you resting?"

Just the mention of sleep produced a yawn that Marjorie cut off with the back of her hand. "You wouldn't believe it. I haven't slept this much since I was a newborn."

"What about Dr. Sam? Have you seen much of him?"

"A few times." The scene from that morning played back in her mind, along with the deplorable things she'd said to him. Once again, Marjorie was struck by her own foolishness.

Lydia paused and closely studied her friend. "What's the matter? You said that as though you don't want anything to do with the man."

"Oh, Sam Bretton is everything you said he was...and more. But to be frank, he simply doesn't interest me."

The perfectly shaped eyebrows above Lydia's dark eyes drew together sharply. "He doesn't interest you?"

"Not really." Marjorie studied her fingernails with feigned interest.

"Do you have a raging fever, girl? Are you stupid? He's wonderful.... He's handsome enough to tempt any red-blooded American woman."

"Not me," Marjorie claimed, her voice gaining conviction. "Nice guy, but not my type."

"He's every woman's type!"

"Maybe." That was as much as Marjorie was willing to concede.

The way Lydia was regarding her, Marjorie had the feeling her friend was considering having her arrested for treason. If she didn't watch it, she'd be dragged before a firing squad at dawn.

"I don't understand you," Lydia said in a low, troubled voice. "The last time I came to visit the scent of a good old-fashioned romance was so thick in this room that I walked away intoxicated. I was convinced you were hooked and would be head over heels in love with him within a week."

"I'm sorry to disappoint you."

"What went wrong?" Lydia crossed her arms, then her legs, and glared at Marjorie as though she'd let a million dollars' worth of gold slip through her fingertips. "When Dr. Sam phoned before the surgery, he sounded...I don't know...interested, I guess. We must have talked a half hour. He asked a hundred questions about you."

"He did?" Marjorie didn't want to hear that.

"I don't know what happened between then and now, but obviously something did."

"I'm his patient," Marjorie insisted, because to do anything else would be ludicrous. That relationship was sacred and not to be tampered with. All afternoon she'd forced herself to view it as something like that of a woman and her priest. It was much safer that way.

"That's too bad," Lydia said with an exaggerated sigh. "I was really hoping things would work out between you two."

"Why?"

"Why?" Lydia repeated, astonished. "Because I think Dr. Sam is the most amazing man I know and because you're my best friend. That's why. The two of you are perfect together."

"You've got to be kidding!" Marjorie cried. Her words resounded throughout the room; the echo taunted her for long hours afterward.

Chapter Four

Marjorie paused just inside the Mercedes show-room and drew a deep breath. It felt wonderful to be back. Wonderful and right. Three weeks recovery time was what Sam had told her she would need, and Marjorie had used every minute of the twenty-one days to recuperate. Even now she felt weak and a little shaky, but the thought of another day holed up in her tiny apartment was enough to make even the most sane person go stir-crazy.

With a sense of appreciation that never waned, Marjorie ran her hand over the trunk of a 560SL roadster. Rarely had she been more eager to get back to work. Bit by bit Marjorie had regained her strength, and now she would quietly resume her life.

"Welcome back," Lydia called eagerly from behind the customer-service counter. "How are you feeling?"

"Terrific, thanks." Marjorie realized her clothes were a little loose and her complexion a bit chalky, but all in all she felt great.

"Has your sister gone back to Oregon?"

Marjorie nodded. Her sister had left a few days before, and it had not been a minute too soon. When Jody had learned about the surgery, there was no stopping the twenty-year-old from coming to her sister's aid. Despite Marjorie's ardent protests, Jody had dropped her studies and immediately driven to Tacoma to play the role of the indulgent nurse. Marjorie loved her sister, but after one entire week of Jody giving an Academy Award performance of Clara Barton, Marjorie had been on the brink of madness.

Within the first hour of her return to Dixon Motors two of the salesmen stopped by her desk to welcome her back. At ten Lydia delivered a cup of coffee, closed the door and pulled out a chair.

"Well?" her co-worker asked, as she plunked herself down and leaned forward anxiously, propping her elbows on the corner of Marjorie's desk. Her eyes were both wide and curious.

Marjorie blinked back her surprise. "Well, what?"

"Did you hear from Dr. Sam?"

"Of course not." With jerky movements Marjorie tore off three weeks, a day at a time, from her desktop calendar.

"Dr. Sam didn't contact you?" Lydia's voice rose dramatically in open disbelief.

"I already told you he didn't." Marjorie had seen Sam exactly twice since that heated episode when she'd accused him of getting a kickback from the hospital. Both times had been strained as Marjorie battled the very strong and very real attraction for him. Again and again she was forced to remind herself that women patients tend to fall in love with their doctors and that she wasn't any more immune to his charms than the rest. Keeping her perspective had been difficult, especially when Sam returned the following day and behaved as though nothing had happened. He had chatted easily with her, but she noted regretfully that he stayed only a few minutes. His second visit had been even shorter.

"That depresses me," Lydia lamented, as she gracefully rose from her chair. "I was convinced he really liked you."

It depressed Marjorie, too, but it didn't surprise her. Overall she was grateful to have met Sam Bretton. He'd taught her several surprising lessons about herself—mainly that she wasn't as invincible as she would like to think. And secondly, as much as she strove to avoid relationships that were more than casual, her heart was vulnerable. He'd proved beyond a doubt that plenty of red-hot blood flowed through her veins.

Painful experience had taught her that most men liked their women soft and clinging. A woman who could change her own oil, balance a checkbook and build a bookshelf seemed to intimidate them. That left the strong, independent types, like herself, out in the cold.

Sam Bretton sat in his office and chewed on the end of a pen. His thoughts were dark and heavy. He hadn't seen Marjorie in more than two weeks, and damn if she didn't pop into his mind when he least expected it. He had seen Marjorie's smile on a new patient's face as he entered the room to introduce himself. His coffee cup had made it halfway to his lips when he thought he heard Marjorie's laugh. Last week he'd been convinced he'd seen her in the parking lot. Even his dreams had been affected. A couple of times he'd caught himself staring into space, remembering something witty she'd said or the way her eyes narrowed when she was angry. Friends had begun to comment that he seemed preoccupied.

Preoccupied! That wasn't the half of it. Forcefully he opened his desk drawer and tossed the pen inside. He'd been thinking about her for days... all right, weeks, and still he wasn't convinced anything between them would work. She was so damnably proud, so headstrong, and he wasn't entirely persuaded she was interested in him. Without being egotistical about it, Sam realized that there were plenty of women who found him attractive. Unfortunately Marjorie didn't appear to be one of them.

Well, he was a big boy, he could deal with that. What was difficult to handle was the fact that he wasn't convinced there could be any future for them. Her streak of independence was a mile wide; she didn't want or need anyone. At least that's what she wanted to think. He just wished he could put her out of his mind.

Expelling a sigh, he leaned back in his chair. But damn if she wasn't the most stimulating woman he'd met in years!

Lydia sat across the table in the deli on the other side of the street from Dixon Motors. Suspiciously she checked between the thick slices of rye bread for the mustard she'd ordered with her pastrami sandwich. "I've been thinking," she muttered under her breath.

"Careful," Marjorie warned, hiding a smile, "that could be dangerous."

"No, I'm serious." Her look gave credence to her words.

"About what?" Marjorie continued to study her friend while she wrapped the second half of her turkey sandwich in a paper napkin to take back to the office for a snack later.

"Didn't you tell me Dr. Sam was interested in buying a Mercedes?"

"I . . . yes, now that you mention it, he did say something along those lines."

The edges of Lydia's mouth quavered with unsuppressed delight. "Then get moving on it, girl! I've never known you to look a gift horse in the mouth."

"I . . ." Marjorie's tongue felt tied to the roof of her mouth.

"If you don't move on this, then you know Al Swanson will."

The arrow hit its mark. Al Swanson was her neme-
sis, and he wouldn't think twice about robbing his own
mother out of a sale. "I'll think about it," Marjorie
said, and gave her friend a bright smile.

Lydia pushed her empty plate aside and stood,
looking pleased with herself. She had the determined
look of someone who planned to get Marjorie and
Sam together even if she had to lock them in a room
herself!

Marjorie checked her watch and was grateful to note
that she was free to leave in fifteen minutes. After her
second day back to work she was eager to get home
and relax. Her afternoon hadn't gone well, and she'd
already crossed Al Swanson when he'd attempted to
undercut a sale. One of her clients had taken out a sedan for a test drive, and when he'd returned, Al had
explained that Marjorie had gone out to lunch and had
asked him to wrap up the deal. Luckily Marjorie had
overheard him and quickly inserted that she was back
and would take over for him.

Incidents like this had happened in the past, and
Marjorie refused to stand for it. She didn't like tat-
tling to the manager, but she wasn't about to let Al
cheat her out of her commission.

The bell chimed as the large double doors opened,
indicating that a customer had entered the showroom. The salespeople took turns dealing with the in-
flux of prospective buyers. She'd only recently
finished helping a young executive, so she left the field
open to Jim Preston, the senior salesman.

"Marjorie," Jim called, and stuck his head in the door. "Someone's here to see you."

Once again, she glanced at her watch. Staying late hadn't been a problem before, but she tired easily now and was eager to head back to her apartment. "Thanks, Jim," she muttered, and pushed herself away from her desk with both hands.

Once in the showroom, Marjorie paused in mid-step and nearly faltered in an effort to disguise her surprise.

"Sam." His name was said in a rush of confusion and delight.

Sam turned away from the light blue convertible. He liked the sleek lines and the classic style of the 560SL, but seventy-five thousand dollars for a car, any car, was more than he cared to spend.

"Hi." Some of Marjorie's composure had returned, and she greeted him with a careful smile. She didn't want to appear overjoyed to see him, although her heart felt as if it were doing somersaults inside her chest.

Sam couldn't take his eyes off her. She looked wonderful. If he'd found her attractive before, it was nothing compared to the way she appeared to him now. To think he'd once pictured this woman as a lost kitten trapped in a storm. This kitten wasn't the ordinary, run-of-the-mill stray. She was of the highest pedigree.

Without even realizing what he was doing, Sam gave a low wolf whistle. He couldn't stop looking at her and finally managed to say, "I see you've recovered."

"You promised I'd live and love again."

Sam grinned and, still a little bemused, rubbed the side of his jaw, unable to carry on the conversation.

Marjorie knew that men found her attractive, but what amused her was the shocked look on Sam's face. "I didn't think the brochure had time to reach you," Marjorie said, her gaze holding Sam's.

"Brochure? What brochure?" He suspected he was beginning to sound like an echo.

"I mailed one off to you yesterday afternoon," she said, and casually crossed her arms over the double-breasted tweed jacket. "You'd mentioned something about wanting a Mercedes, and I extended an invitation for you to come in and take a test drive."

"I'd enjoy that," Sam murmured, glancing toward the sticker on the side window of the car he'd been inspecting.

"Perhaps it would be best if I explained the different models," Marjorie continued, her gaze following his. "Our cars start in the range of thirty thousand dollars," she said in an even, smooth voice, "depending, of course, on the options you decide upon."

"Naturally."

Leading the way into her office, she turned back and asked, "Would you care for a cup of coffee?"

"Please."

Marjorie's thoughts were racing as she directed him into her cubicle. From the corner of her eye she happened to catch a glimpse of Lydia, who flashed her a triumphant grin and the universal signal for okay.

Once Sam was comfortably seated, she'd poured coffee in a Styrofoam cup and handed it to him. Although she remained outwardly poised, her heart was pumping blood so fast, she felt dizzy and a little shaky. She knew her face was flushed.

When Marjorie was dealing with a prospective buyer, she usually approached them with an angle. This involved asking a few subtle, but pertinent questions and discovering their individual concerns. Some potential buyers were looking at a Mercedes for performance—the German-made automobile was built to cruise at twice the speed of U.S. freeways. Marjorie realized, though, that Sam wasn't interested in traveling over a hundred miles an hour. From what she did know about Sam, he wasn't the type who cared a great deal about prestige, either. The safety issue would evoke a response in him.

"The Mercedes-Benz is the safest car made in the world." She handed him a brochure from her desk drawer and took her seat. "Air bags are standard equipment on every car we sell."

"I remember reading about those," Sam said, and watched her with renewed interest. As a car saleswoman, she was as slick as frost on mossy rocks. Yes, she was a beautiful woman, but once she had a customer's attention it was cars she was there to sell.

"I like to tell prospective buyers that purchasing a Mercedes-Benz is another form of life insurance," Marjorie continued. "As a physician, I'm sure you can appreciate the many safety features."

Sam flipped through the pages of the glossy pamphlet and nodded. She knew her stuff, he had to give her credit for that. "You're very good."

Marjorie paused. "How do you mean?"

"As a salesman."

"Salesperson," she corrected with a smile.

"I don't think many men would be able to turn you down."

A couple of the salesmen had protested that very matter when Marjorie was first hired, claiming she had an unfair advantage over the others. Sitting across the table from a good-looking female, a man would have a difficult time negotiating a price. The men might have convinced a few of the others they had a point, but Bud, the manager, was behind Marjorie. Her sales record spoke for itself. She sold cars, and that was the purpose of the dealership. If she possessed an unfair advantage, the manager didn't care as long as cars moved out of the lot. Marjorie didn't use her feminine wiles; the cars sold because she was a good salesperson.

"I get turned down often," Marjorie responded, her smile fading.

Sam turned the page of the brochure and read over the information on the 300E model. "I'll take this one."

"Pardon." Marjorie wasn't completely sure she had heard him right.

"This sedan—in a light blue if you have it."

"You mean you want to buy one now?"

"Is that a problem?" He withdrew his checkbook from inside his coat pocket.

Marjorie had sold dozens of cars, but never any quite this way. "Don't you want to negotiate the price?"

"Not particularly. I know you aren't going to cheat me."

"But…" Experience told her to shut up. She didn't need to kill a sale by arguing with him. Marjorie clamped her mouth closed and swallowed her questions. Sam was an adult; he knew what he wanted. Far be it from her to stand in his way.

"I trust you to be fair," the good doctor continued, adding the pertinent details to the blank check. "How much should I fill in for the amount?"

Hours later Marjorie was still completely bemused. She wandered around her apartment, moving from room to room, listless and bored and, at the same time, excited. She'd seen Sam again, and even if he had come into the showroom to buy a car and not just to see her, she was thrilled. At the same time she regretted the encounter. Knowing that other patients fell in love with him had been reassuring, but to her dismay Marjorie learned that the attraction she'd experienced for Sam hadn't lessened with time. It had been weeks since she'd last seen him, and he looked better to her than ever. All the emotions she'd struggled so valiantly to bury had surfaced the minute she'd walked into the showroom to discover him standing there. All

the pleasure of seeing him again returned to remind
her how strongly Sam Bretton appealed to her.

When Sam Bretton walked into Dixon Motors the
following morning, every word that Marjorie had re-
hearsed so carefully, every scenario she'd spent hours
plotting fell by the wayside. All she could see was the
gentle, kind man who had sat at her bedside and held
her hand.

"Hello, Sam." It was amazing that she'd been able
to utter those few words. She trembled inside. No
longer was she an inept hospital patient, but a woman
who knew what she liked—and Sam Bretton was it.
The thought terrified her.

"Hello, again."

"Everything's ready." She straightened the French
cuffs of her sleeves, bemoaning the fact that everything she owned was either blue, black or gray. It
wasn't any wonder dates were few and far between.
She resembled Lee Iacocca more than Madonna.

Marjorie swallowed her self-doubts and gestured
toward the customer-service counter. "Lydia will need
you to fill out a few forms."

Sam looked mildly surprised, but he followed Marjorie into the other office. Lydia greeted him with a
wide smile, and Sam was left with the impression that
he'd done something very right to have gained her
undying gratitude.

Buying the Mercedes couldn't have been any less
obvious even to Marjorie. Against his better judg-
ment he'd decided he wanted to see her again. He'd

planned on getting a luxury car someday, and now seemed as good a time as any. Besides, he wanted Marjorie to have this sale. He remembered her telling him once how she lived on commissions alone. This was his way of helping her through what was sure to be a difficult month, since the first three weeks had been spent recuperating from surgery. He had decided against negotiating the price.

While Sam was with Lydia, Marjorie stood on the showroom floor, pacing back and forth while she waited for him to finish with Lydia. Her hands felt damp, her throat dry, and yet to all outward appearances she was as cool as a pumpkin on a frosty October morning.

When Sam was finished, she approached him with a grin and handed him the keys to his shiny new 300E sedan, which she'd arranged to have waiting for him in front of the dealership.

"That didn't take long," she said, as a means of starting a conversation. From experience she knew the paperwork wouldn't take more than ten or fifteen minutes.

"Have you got time to take a spin with me?" Sam invited.

She nodded, hoping she didn't appear as eager as she felt. "Of course."

Like the true gentleman he was, Sam held open the passenger door for her, and she gracefully slipped inside. He joined her a moment later, inserted the key into the ignition and paused to inhale the fresh scent of new leather and study the dials in front of him.

It was on the tip of Marjorie's tongue to give him another sales pitch and quote what *Car and Driver* and *Auto Motor and Sport* had to say about the 300E sedan. She knew her stuff, but the sale had already been made, and he only had to drive the German-made vehicle to be impressed.

Wordlessly Sam eased the sedan into the busy Tacoma traffic, quickly acquainting himself with the mechanics of the car. They rode past the digital signboard that twisted above the Puget Sound Bank.

"Actually, you being able to pick up the car this morning works rather well," Marjorie said.

"How's that?" Sam looked away from traffic long enough to glance in her direction.

"I can treat you to lunch." As soon as the words slipped from her lips, Marjorie was flabbergasted. She didn't know where the invitation had come from.

"Marjorie..."

"That is unless you can't...I mean, if you're due back at the office...The reason I asked is that I always treat new customers to lunch. It's my way of showing my appreciation for your business." Marjorie was convinced these lies would someday return to haunt her.

"But I was thinking of taking you out."

"I owe you this one," she insisted. "For the car, yes, and everything else."

"You're a difficult woman to refuse."

How Marjorie wished that were true. "How do you like Mexican food?"

"Love it. But, Marjorie, I would prefer it if you allowed me to buy lunch."

"You'd break tradition." Marjorie was convinced her nose would start growing at any minute.

Sam grinned. The more he came to know this woman, the more he learned about pride. "Are you always so stubborn?"

"Always," she answered evenly, and pointed to the left-hand side of the street. "The restaurant is about a block farther. There's parking on the street and a small lot around back."

Sam parked easily. Once inside, they were forced to put their name on a list, but Marjorie assured him the food was well worth the wait. They were seated within ten minutes; the waitress seemed to know Marjorie.

"Do you come here often?"

She nodded and finished munching on a warm tortilla chip before answering. "At least once a week. I'm worthless in the kitchen, and it's healthier for me to eat out."

Sam's insides tightened. He should have guessed that Marjorie would be a terrible cook, and he felt almost guilty because it bothered him so much. The woman he was looking to build his life with should possess at least the rudimentary culinary skills.

"The last time I experimented with a recipe," Marjorie continued, "I set off the fire alarm and cleared the entire apartment complex. Under direct orders of the building manager and the Tacoma Fire Department, I've been asked to refrain from any kitchen activities."

The sound of Sam's strained chuckle mingled with the chatter in the small restaurant.

"My sister swears that I'll make someone a wonderful husband." In many ways what Jody claimed was true; Marjorie could fix just about anything. But cooking and sewing were lost arts to her.

Sam found the food to be as good as Marjorie had claimed. He watched her eat with undisguised gusto and then pause, obviously embarrassed, to explain that she was only now regaining her appetite.

As she dabbed a drop of hot sauce from the corner of her mouth with a paper napkin, Marjorie's gaze fell to her empty plate. No doubt most women Sam dated were dainty things who ate like sparrows and fit in extra-petite panty hose. She downed the remainder of her Mexican beer, equally sure she'd done the wrong thing by ordering it. Sam's women probably drank tea diluted with milk. For once in her life Marjorie wished she could be different. She wanted Sam to like her even with her healthy appetite and appreciation of good beer.

The waitress returned for their plates and served two cups of coffee. Sam noted the sudden lag in the conversation and picked it up easily, entertaining her with anecdotes from his youth.

Marjorie was so engrossed in his stories that when she happened to check her watch, she saw that it was one-forty-five.

"Oh, Sam, I've got an appointment at two." A stockbroker was coming in to test-drive a 300SDL sedan, and she couldn't be late.

They hurried out of the restaurant, and Sam had her back at the dealership with minutes to spare. Even though her customer was due to arrive at any time, Marjorie was reluctant to part. She turned back, her hand on the car door, wanting to tell him so many things and not knowing where to start.

"Thank you, Sam," she said softly. That seemed so inadequate. "It seems I'm always having to thank you for one reason or another. Have you noticed that?"

"No," he answered evenly. "Besides, I should be the one thanking you."

"It was only lunch." And she owed him so much more than a simple meal. He'd given her another argument when the tab arrived, but she'd won. She realized now that it probably would have been better if she'd let him pay—male pride being what it is. Everything had gone incredibly wrong this afternoon...and incredibly right.

"Next time it's my turn."

Marjorie was outside the car before his words registered. "Right," she answered, and a broad smile grew and grew.

He gestured with his hand. "Bye, Marjorie."

"Bye, Sam." She waited until he'd driven away and was out of sight before she entered the dealership.

No sooner had she stepped onto the showroom floor, than Lydia appeared. "Where in heaven's name did the two of you take off to? You've been gone for hours! Where'd you go? Did he ask you out again? I told you he was interested. Remember what I said?"

"We went to lunch."

Lydia nodded approvingly. "I bet he took you to a fancy place on the waterfront that serves lobster."

Marjorie had a difficult time containing her amusement. "Actually, I treated him at The Lindo."

"That Mexican place you're always bragging about?"

"The food's wonderful."

"And you paid?"

"I...I told him I do that with all first-time car buyers."

Lydia's frown relaxed into a soft, encouraging smile. "Hey, not a bad idea."

"He said he'd treat next time." Marjorie cast her gaze longingly toward the street. "Do you think he'll phone?" She hated feeling so insecure, but more than anything else, she wanted to see Sam again.

"I bet you ten dollars he calls by tomorrow."

Lydia lost the bet.

Two days later Marjorie had chewed off two fingernails and was quickly becoming a nervous wreck. She'd never been a patient person, and waiting for Sam to contact her was slowly but surely driving her crazy.

"You aren't going to sit still for this, are you?" Lydia said over lunch.

"What other choice do I have?"

"Oh, come on, Marjorie!" Lydia declared, crumpling her napkin and tossing it atop her empty plate. "I've watched you chase after a sale when anyone else would have given it up. You have a reputation for putting deals together when others would have thrown their hands in the air.''

"Yes, but selling cars and dealing with a man are two entirely different matters.''

"No they're not," Lydia disagreed sharply.

"You think I should phone him?" The idea didn't appeal to her. Sam had left her with the impression that he'd contact her.

"No..." Lydia gazed thoughtfully at the ceiling fixture while working her bottom lip between two fingers. "You need a more subtle approach.''

"I suppose I could do what he did,'' Marjorie murmured thoughtfully.

Lydia's stare was blank. "What do you mean?''

"Meet him on his own ground. I could call for an appointment, claim I was having problems with the insurance papers or something.''

Lydia nearly tipped back the chair in her enthusiasm. "That's perfect, and nothing would appear out of the ordinary for you to show up with the forms.''

Even though it sounded easy, it took Marjorie nearly all afternoon to work up the courage to contact Sam's office. Since she feared the receptionist would probably handle any insurance work, Marjorie asked for an appointment and was given one later the following week. Now that she'd taken some positive action, Marjorie felt a hundred times better—until she saw Lydia's shocked face later that same afternoon.

"What's the matter?''

"Dr. Sam's office just called.''

"And?''

"And well . . . apparently Dr. Sam looked over his schedule and saw your name."

"And?"

"Marjorie, I'm sure there's a logical explanation."

"Lydia, for heaven's sake, will you stop beating around the bush and tell me what's going on?"

"You know Mary and I are good friends, don't you?"

From what she remembered, Mary was Sam's receptionist. "Yes, what did she say?"

"Mary told me that when Dr. Sam saw your name, he became upset, swore under his breath and asked Mary to call you and suggest you make an appointment with another doctor."

Chapter Five

Marjorie turned on the television, impatiently jerked around and plunked herself down on the overstuffed sofa, crossing her arms in a defiant gesture. Five minutes later she charged out of her seat and rushed across the room to switch channels. She was as mad as hops, and the hope of a mere television movie salving her injured ego was nil.

Men! Sam Bretton in particular! None of them were worth all this aggravation. Marjorie had behaved like a fool over the good physician, and knowing it made her lack of savoir faire all the more difficult to swallow.

Hindsight nearly always proved to be twenty-twenty, but Marjorie should have known not to trust a man who preferred mild salsa sauce on his enchiladas. If he couldn't eat a jalapeño straight from the jar, he wasn't her type. Marjorie liked her food and her men spicy and pungent. Sam was too...too wonderful. That was it, much too wonderful.

Depression settled over her shoulders like a dark mantle, and she rubbed her forearms to ward off a late-evening chill that had little to do with the mild Puget Sound weather. Sam and she were simply too different. Sam liked moonlight walks and a glass of wine in front of the fireplace, and she liked... moonlight walks and a glass of wine in front of the fireplace. Damn, going over every detail a hundred times wasn't going to settle anything. He didn't want to see her again, and that was that.

All right, she was an adult, she should be able to handle disappointments. Obviously Sam was interested in meek, mild women who knew their place. Marjorie was neither, and it was far easier to have faced the situation now than later when her heart was infected and the prognosis for recovery would be against her.

Once Marjorie had sorted through her myriad thoughts, she felt better, even good enough to put this unpleasantness behind her and think about fixing herself something to eat. She left the television on and wandered into the kitchen. The freezer contained a wide assortment of cardboard meals, but she wasn't in the mood for anything that elaborate. Popcorn suited her mood—something crunchy and salty that would help to vent some frustration. Microwave popcorn, naturally. What she'd told Sam about her lack of expertise in the kitchen had been true. Spreadsheets and calculators could be managed in her sleep, but recipes and sewing patterns baffled her. Having her anywhere in the vicinity of hot grease was like putting a submachine gun in the hands of a raw recruit. In fact she didn't even own a complete set of cookware. In an effort to appease the apartment manager after her last cooking fiasco, Marjorie had personally handed over the last of her pots and pans. The less she involved herself with a stove top, the better.

Opening her microwave, Marjorie inserted the popcorn bag, set the timer and waited. Soon the sounds and smells of the butter-flavored kernels filled the small apartment.

She had just opened the bag and munched down the first handful when the doorbell chimed. A glance at the wall clock told her it was after nine. She certainly wasn't expecting anyone. The hope that it might be Sam caused her to hurry. It wouldn't be Sam—Marjorie consciously realized that—but she so wanted to see him again that her mind tormented her with the possibility.

With an eagerness that was difficult to explain, Marjorie opened her front door. Sam stood on the other side. It was as though her wishful thinking had conjured up the good doctor.

"Hello, Sam." She greeted him as though she'd been expecting him all along, revealing no surprise.

He looked terrible. Exhausted, overworked and not quite himself. She would have thought Sam would never allow a strand of hair to fall out of place, but his hair wasn't the only thing rumpled; everything about him looked unkempt. His clothes hung on him, the top two buttons of his shirt were unfastened. He hadn't shaved in a couple of days, or so it appeared.

"I have had the worst day of my life," Sam announced, walking past her and into the apartment.

Bemused, Marjorie remained at the entrance, her hand on the doorknob. She'd expected contrition, guilt, grief, but not this out-and-out appeal for sympathy.

"It's been one thing after another," he continued undaunted. Without invitation, he picked up her *TV Guide* and flipped through the entertainment section for that evening.

"Would you like something to drink?" she offered, choosing to ignore his outburst.

"Please." He sank onto her sofa and leaned forward to wipe the tiredness from his eyes. He'd planned on calling Marjorie hours earlier and inviting her to dinner. Before he could get to a phone, Betty Brightfield had gone into labor, and he'd spent the next five hours at the hospital with her. The delivery had been difficult, and he hadn't been able to get away until now. The unexpected trip to the delivery room and the arrival of Baby Brightfield had been a climax to a long, tedious day.

Sam realized that arriving unannounced on Marjorie's doorstep probably wasn't one of his most brilliant ideas, but he wanted to straighten out a few things between them, and delaying the discussion was potentially unwise. He was beginning to know Marjorie Majors, and the message she was bound to read into the canceled appointment would be all wrong.

Marjorie went into her kitchen to survey her meager supply of refreshments. All she could find was a two-liter bottle of flat cola in the back of her refrigerator, a can of tomato juice with a rusty crust over the aluminum top and a carton of milk she'd been meaning to toss for the past week.

"Is instant coffee all right?"

"Fine, fine." He really didn't care for anything but a long talk with Marjorie. He leaned back and inhaled deeply, paused, then added, "Do I smell popcorn?"

Grinning, Marjorie stuck her head around the corner of her kitchen. Nothing smelled better than freshly popped popcorn. "Want some?"

Sam shook his head. "No, thanks. I haven't had any dinner."

"This is my dinner."

His face twisted into a mock scowl that revealed his amusement. Naturally she was joking with him. "You're kidding, right?"

"No."

Sam jumped up from the couch with a reserve of energy he hadn't realized he possessed. "You can't eat that for dinner... it's unhealthy."

"I disagree." Everything she'd read contradicted Sam. The kernels were reported to be a good source of fiber in the diet, and since she ate her main meal at noon, it made sense to have something light in the evenings.

"Don't you know you're not supposed to argue with a doctor?" Actually, Sam wasn't as concerned about the nutritional value of popcorn as he was that her choice for her evening meal gave him an excellent excuse to invite her out.

"Sam, it isn't any big deal..."

"Come on, I'll take you to dinner."

Marjorie hedged. "But you just said today's been the worst day of your life. What you need is to put up your feet and enjoy a good home-cooked meal." Oh, heavens, why had she suggested that? Sam would assume she'd do the cooking, and then there'd be real trouble. She might be able to bluff her way through some things, but a complete meal was out of the question.

The idea of Marjorie preparing a meal for him appealed to Sam, but he studied her carefully. Maybe he'd misunderstood her earlier. "You told me you don't cook."

At that moment Marjorie would have gladly surrendered three commissions to Al Swanson to have possessed the ability to whip together a three-egg cheese-and-mushroom omelet, but she knew better than to offer. She'd given her word of honor to her landlord not to do anything unnecessary in the kitchen. Still, the temptation was so strong. She opened her mouth and closed it again. "I make excellent microwave popcorn," she offered weakly, and gestured toward the open bag sitting on the counter behind her.

"Then popcorn it is," Sam said, lowering himself into a sitting position. While he waited, he glanced at the television and recognized an old-fashioned romance from the late fifties. He wouldn't have thought Marjorie would appreciate anything that was this sentimental. But then she'd surprised him before.

"Here's your coffee and dinner. It's the special of the house." She brought in a steaming cup and handed it to him and a breadbasket filled with hot popcorn. "I'll be back in a minute."

"I owe you a dinner, you know."

"As I recall, it's a lunch, and if you're counting that, you might as well add a movie and popcorn to the list." He didn't owe her anything. Not really—she was the one in debt. Sam had given her so much more than she could ever hope to repay.

He relaxed against the thick cushions and felt his body release a silent sigh of relief. He'd missed Marjorie over the past couple of days. Missed her wit. Missed her warmth. Missed her smile. He'd wanted to see her again despite his reservations. For two days he'd been trying to find the time to call her, but there was never more than those odd five minutes here or ten minutes there. Besides, what he had to say would be better said in person. There was too much room for misunderstanding over the phone. Letting another day pass without seeing Marjorie would only add to his mounting frustration.

She joined him a minute later, stretched her legs on top of the coffee table and crossed them at the ankles. Judging exactly where she should sit had been a problem. If she sat too close, he might read something into that. On the other hand, if she positioned herself as far away as possible, he might think she didn't want him around. Nothing could be farther from the truth.

They sat quietly for a moment, then Marjorie ventured into conversation. "So your day went badly?"

"Not completely. A first baby and, as sometimes happens, I had a difficult delivery."

Even as she tried not to, Marjorie started laughing. "*You* went through a difficult delivery? How's the poor mother doing?"

"Better than me, I think. She got her girl."

"And what did you get?"

The same reward that came with every new life he brought into the world—pride and a deep sense of satisfaction.

"Plenty," he answered, in a gentle way that assured her that no matter what problems he faced, he was content with his life.

The unexpected vision of Marjorie with a baby, their baby in her arms produced such an intense longing that his breath jammed in his lungs. He shook his head to dispel the image, but it remained, clearer than before. For years Sam had brought children into the world. He'd spent countless hours encouraging new mothers and an equal amount of time soothing soon-to-be fathers, but only rarely had he thought about the woman who would give him children.

Their eyes met, and Sam's smile embraced her. She didn't know what he was thinking, but had she been holding her coffee cup it would have slipped from her fingers. Sam had the most sensuous smile of any man she'd ever known.

"How have you been?"

"Good." She nodded once. "You?"

"Fine."

Marjorie swallowed and headed for the deep end. "About that appointment..."

"Yes, I wanted to talk to you about that."

"I got the insurance papers straightened out—no problem."

"Insurance papers? You made the appointment to go over some papers?" Sam felt like a heel now. He thought she'd wanted a physical or something else equally impossible.

Her excuse to see him sounded so flimsy in the light of their conversation that a deep flush crept up her neck and over her ears.

"It would be best if you got another physician," Sam said, and cleared his throat. "I'd be more than happy to recommend one if you want."

Marjorie couldn't believe what she was hearing. He said it so calmly, without so much as a hint of regret, as though they were discussing the weather or something equally trivial. In so few words he was telling her he wanted her out of his life.

Unable to trust her voice, she nodded.

"It's important for everyone to have a regular physician," Sam insisted. "Cal Johnson will be doing the follow-up with the surgery, and it would be better for both of us if you went to him. But he's a surgeon, and you need a general practitioner."

Marjorie's throat closed up on her, the tightness making it difficult to breathe evenly.

The wounded look in her eyes tore at Sam's heart. It was apparent that she still didn't understand. He'd have to spell it out for her.

"I think you're wonderful, Marjorie."

Sure he did. Enough to dump her in her greatest hour of need.

"I'd like to see a lot more of you," Sam continued, "and I can't do that if you continue to be my patient."

Marjorie jerked her head around. What had he said? He wanted to see her—as in date her? Spend time with her? Be with her? She blinked and pointed her index finger at her chest. "You want to see more of me?"

"Don't look so surprised."

"I'm not.... It's just that..."

"It shouldn't seem all that sudden. You must have known in the hospital I was interested. Believe me, I don't spend that much time with all my patients."

"I know, but...I don't know..." She was unsure, confused. Her gaze narrowed as she studied him. It would be best to clear away any misconceptions up front. "It's not gratitude, you know."

"It's not?" He didn't quite follow her meaning.

"Of course I'm grateful for everything you've done, but if we'd met on the street, I'd have felt the same things I do now."

"Which are?" he prompted, scooting closer to her. His dark, round eyes surveyed her with renewed interest.

"Never mind," Marjorie said with a small laugh. She could see no reason to bolster his ego any higher than it was already.

With his eyes steadily holding hers, Sam tucked a finger beneath her chin and slowly raised her mouth to his. Marjorie's eyelids fluttered closed as she awaited the warm sensation of his lips settling over hers. Sam didn't keep her waiting long. His arms encircled her, drawing her gently against his hard chest.

Their lips met in an unrushed exploration, as though they had all the time in the world and there wasn't any reason to hurry anything. His mouth was moist and pliant against her own, moving with such gentleness, such care that a tiny shudder worked its way through Marjorie, and with it came a helpless moan.

After torturous seconds Sam's lips reluctantly left hers. He buried his face in the curve of her shoulder and inhaled a calming breath. He'd felt physically drained when he'd arrived. Now he was alive, more alive than he could ever remember being. Holding Marjorie, touching her energized him, filled him with purpose, exhilarated him, eased the ache of loneliness that followed whenever he returned to an empty house after a delivery.

The wealth of sensation took Marjorie by surprise. A simple kiss—their first—had left her with a hunger as deep as the sea. Emotion clogged her throat, and she held him to her, her fingers weaving the thick strands of his dark hair.

"Marjorie?"

"Hmm?"

"Do you always smell this good?"

Her eyes remained closed, and she grinned. "I think it's the popcorn."

"Not this. It's roses, I think."

"My perfume."

"Sunshine."

"I showered when I got home."

He shook his head, declining her explanation. "And something more, something I can't define."

"That's probably the popcorn."

Sam shook his head. "Not this," he countered softly. "Not this."

The reluctance with which Sam loosened his hold thrilled Marjorie. They straightened and went back to watching the movie. He tucked his arm around her, and she pressed her head against his shoulder. The warmth of his nearness convinced her that the man beside her was indeed real and not the product of a fanciful imagination or some anesthetic-induced illusion.

A multitude of unanswered questions ran through her thoughts. It was on the tip of her tongue to blurt out everything she felt for him, but she feared ruining this special evening.

"So you enjoy old movies," he said, the thought pleasing him.

"Especially the classics. They did romances so well in those days."

"You like romance?"

Marjorie nodded and hid a smile. "I'm liking it more all the time."

"I am, too," Sam agreed, and turned her toward him. He wanted to kiss her again, taste her sweetness and experience once again that special power she possessed that filled him with such energy.

It was a long time before Marjorie saw any more of the movie. Or cared.

Chapter Six

You aren't going to let Al get away with it, are you?'' Lydia cried in outrage, indignation flushing her cheeks.

Marjorie didn't need to be angry about Al Swanson's latest attempt to steal a customer from her; Lydia was furious enough for the both of them. "Bud will be the one to decide.''

"But you know Al is lying.''

"It's my word against his, and unfortunately Bud's only the manager, not Solomon.''

"But it's so unfair.''

"Tell me about it,'' Marjorie grumbled. Once again Al had tried to horn in on her deal. Only this time he'd succeeded. Marjorie had spoken to a couple about a 190E 2.6 sedan, worked with them, called the couple twice to keep them interested and even rode with them as they test-drove four different Mercedes models in order to answer their numerous questions. The middle-aged pair had gone home to sleep on the decision and returned the following day with a deposit. Al had met them at the door, claimed Marjorie had stepped out of the office, and they had asked him to write up the deal on her behalf. This was the same trick he'd used once before, only this time it worked. Once the paperwork was firmly clenched in his hand, Marjorie hadn't a leg to stand on. She had complained to the manager, insisted she had been at the dealership and not out, as Al had alleged. Since Bud had been gone and there wasn't anyone to verify her story, things didn't look good for her. But the manager wasn't completely naive when it came to Al. He'd heard complaints from one or two of the other salespeople. Bud's fair assessment of the situation was Marjorie's only real hope. Unfortunately Al's name was on the paperwork.

The commission scale was based on the profit margin the dealership made with the sale of each new car. Marjorie collected thirty percent of the capital gain. In this case she'd worked hard to give the couple the best deal possible. Her share was meager enough. If forced to split her commission with Al, Marjorie would have worked long, hard hours for practically nothing. Everything rested on Bud's decision.

"But Bud doesn't know Al the way we do," Lydia continued insistently.

Marjorie studied her friend and was hard-pressed to hold back her own indignation. Al might think he was getting away with something, but if she had anything to do with it, the cheating salesman would spend the next fifty years regretting his underhandedness. Given enough rope, Al Swanson was bound to hang himself sooner or later, and Marjorie hoped she was around to see it happen.

"If he's tried those things with me, he'll do it with the others," Marjorie said thoughtfully after a while. Yes, she was furious, but losing her cool wouldn't solve anything.

"It's the meantime that I'm worried about," Lydia mumbled, crossing her arms and righteously puffing out her chest. "When's Bud going to let you know?"

Marjorie glanced at her watch. "As soon as he gets in."

The low hum of the intercom caught their attention. "Marjorie, call on line three. Marjorie—line three."

"I better get that," Marjorie mumbled, and sighed. "It could mean another sale."

"Not if Al can get his greedy hands on it," Lydia added sourly, and returned to her place behind the customer-service counter.

With her friend's words ringing in her ears, Marjorie walked over to her office and reached for the phone. "Marjorie Majors," she said in a cordial, businesslike tone.

"Dr. Sam Bretton here," Sam returned.

Pulling the chair out from her desk, Marjorie sat down and propped her elbows on the desktop. A rush of pleasure washed over her, taking with it some of the bitter aftertaste of Al's trickery. "Hello."

"I was just thinking about you."

"Oh?" Marjorie knew that she sounded about as intelligent as mold, but he'd taken her by surprise.

"I just returned from the hospital, and my first appointment isn't scheduled for another five minutes, so I thought I'd give you a call. You don't mind, do you?"

"No...it's a pleasant surprise."

"How's your day going?"

"Fair." It would have been much better if the air were cleared between her and Al, but none of this mess was Sam's problem. "How about your morning?"

"Hectic, as always." Actually, he'd been preoccupied, thinking about Marjorie and angry with himself for not setting a date with her. He'd left her apartment feeling exhilarated and excited. They'd sat and talked long after the movie had finished, easily drifting from one subject to another. Marjorie was well-read and knowledgeable in current affairs. He'd found her opinions insightful and intelligent and marveled that he'd found a woman who stirred his heart as well as his mind. So she didn't cook and couldn't sew; he could deal with that. He enjoyed Marjorie's company, relished their time together and longed to see her again soon. Unfortunately his head had been in the clouds, and he hadn't made a date. He'd tried calling her apartment, but she'd already left for work. He knew she worked odd hours and decided his best chance of catching her was at Dixon's. He didn't want to wait another two days to see her again.

"I suppose I should apologize for last night," she said softly.

"Why?" Something was wrong. Sam could detect the subtle difference in her voice. Whatever it was, he hoped she would share it with him.

"I feel bad about not being able to offer you anything more appetizing than microwave popcorn."

"I can't remember when I've enjoyed a meal more."

Marjorie was sure that couldn't be true. No doubt there were a thousand nurses out there who longed to lure him into their arms with hot chocolate-chip cookies straight from the oven. Her microwave couldn't hope to compete with all the talented, domestic women who wanted him.

"Are you free tonight?" Sam asked, thinking about taking her to the waterfront for a lobster dinner. He wanted to wine and dine her and give her an evening she'd remember the rest of her life. He thought about bringing her to his home and showing her his view of Commencement Bay. He wanted to sit by the fireplace with her and watch the flickering light dance over her sweet face.

"Tonight?" she asked, confused by the unexpected invitation.

Sooner, if possible, Sam thought, but he knew his schedule wouldn't allow it.

"Actually, I'm working late, so maybe..."

"What time do you get off?"

She wished he wasn't so insistent. With Bud's decision hanging over her head, she needed some time alone to clear her thoughts. When she was with Sam, she wanted to look and feel her best. "Would it be all right if I called you next week sometime?"

Sam's breath caught at the implication. There wasn't a woman alive who threw him off course with as much ease as Marjorie. Just when he was prepared to overlook her flaws and lay his heart at her feet, she made it sound as though going to dinner with him were an inconvenience.

"Sure," he returned flippantly. "You call me. That won't be any problem."

But it was, and Marjorie recognized it from his stiff tone. She had just opened her mouth to explain when he spoke again.

"Listen, I've got to get back to my patients. We'll talk soon." Sam was eager to get off the phone. The entire conversation had left a bad taste in his mouth. He'd read Marjorie wrong, read everything wrong. It wasn't the first time she'd led him astray. The stock market was more predictable than Marjorie Majors.

"Right." But her voice was barely audible. "Goodbye, Sam. Thanks for calling."

He didn't answer, and Marjorie bit her bottom lip to keep from shouting that she'd love to see him any night, any time, if only she didn't have this mess with Al to settle first. The phone line was disconnected, and Marjorie felt physically ill. She'd ruined everything.

The polite knock outside her office lifted Marjorie from the pits of despair.

"It's only me," Lydia said, opening the door and peeking inside. "Hey, you look like you just lost your best friend. What happened? Another deal fall through?"

The words congealed in Marjorie's throat, and it took a few moments for her to unscramble her thoughts. "That was Sam."

"Dr. Sam?"

It was all Marjorie could do to nod. "I blew it."

"Oh, good grief," Lydia cried. "Not again."

Marjorie dropped her gaze to the floor. "I'm afraid so."

"What did you do this time?"

"He suggested we get together tonight, and I said I was busy and that it would be better if I contacted him."

A moment of stunned silence followed.

"You didn't! Tell me you didn't say that!" Lydia marched into the room and pressed both hands on top of Marjorie's desk, leaning forward so that their faces were scant inches apart. "If the two of you ever get together, I swear it will be a miracle. Good grief, what made you put him off that way?"

"I don't know. This thing with Al's really got me down, and I wanted Sam to see me at my best...not my worst."

Lydia closed her eyes and slowly shook her head. "I've got more bad news for you."

"What's that?"

"Bud's here," Lydia announced starkly. "And he's in one hell of a bad mood. He wants to see you right away."

Even before Marjorie left the dealership at a quarter after nine, she knew she wasn't heading home. Sam's Brown's Point address was tucked safely away in her purse, and she had every intention of talking to him before she did anything. Maybe she could undo some of the damage.

She located the house without a problem, pulled into the wide driveway and turned off her engine. Sam's home was a magnificent sprawling ranch house made of used brick. Huge picture windows faced the street.

Marjorie's heart was pounding like a locomotive chugging uphill. Now she understood what courage it had taken for Sam to arrive unannounced at her apartment! She didn't often do this sort of thing, and swallowing her pride made it all the more difficult.

While her conviction held, she climbed out of the car and marched up to his front door like a soldier making his way to the front of a firing squad. Her hand faltered as she rang the bell.

Marjorie heard Sam's footsteps long before the door was opened. "Marjorie." He blinked, certain she was a figment of his imagination.

"I know I should have called...."

"No," he said, and smiled that slow, sexy smile of his as he stepped aside. "Come in, please."

Relieved by his warm welcome, she entered his home. The first thing that she noticed when Sam led her into the huge, tiled entryway was the large, unobstructed view of Commencement Bay from the floor-to-ceiling living-room windows. The twinkling lights of barges and ferryboats lit up the inky black night and reflected off the water.

"Oh, Sam," she said, her voice low in wondrous awe. "This is so beautiful... it's marvelous." Words failed her, and she blinked away the tears that sprang so readily to the surface when she was confronted with such unrestrained natural beauty.

"I love it, too." He didn't know what had brought her here—didn't care. She'd been on his mind all day. Sam regretted the abrupt way in which he'd ended their telephone conversation, and all because his fragile ego had been pricked. Most of the evening had been spent trying to come up with a way to see Marjorie again and preserve both their prides.

"Sam," she said, tearing her gaze from the water and turning in order to face him. Her features were strained with an expression of practiced poise. "I've come to apologize for this morning."

"No," he countered quickly, sensing her apprehension. "I should be the one to do that." Her appealing gaze cut a path straight to his heart. His own features were tightly controlled.

"You?" she said, and laughed shortly. "But I was the one who was rude."

"Something was troubling you. I knew it the minute you spoke." He longed to ease whatever it was that was bothering her and kicked himself more than once for having been such a fool.

Her eyes narrowed as she studied him. If Sam found her so readable, it would be difficult to hide anything from him.

"Come in and relax," Sam offered, leading her into the living room. The white leather couch was L-shaped, and decorated with several huge pillows in brilliant shades of blue to complement the plush carpet.

Marjorie sat and her gaze drifted once more to the panoramic view of Commencement Bay. Just being here with Sam soothed her. All day she'd been battling her resentment toward Al and what the loss of this commission would mean to her already strained budget.

"Do you want to tell me about it?" Sam asked, taking a seat beside her.

Marjorie nodded. "I owe you that much at least." For the next half hour she explained what had happened with Al and how his devious methods had cheated her out of half the commission on the sale of the 190E sedan. By the time she'd finished, Sam had stood and was pacing in front of the coffee table with barely restrained anger. The corners of his mouth were pinched and white, his hands knotted in tight fists.

"What's being done about this?" he demanded.

"Nothing."

"Nothing?" Sam raged.

"The decision's already been made."

"But he lied."

"I know that and so does nearly everyone else, but it's his name on the contract, so he's entitled to a commission no matter how much time I spent with those people. At least my protest to the manager earned me half of it. That's the way things are done in sales."

It had been a long time since Sam had felt this angry. He would like to find Marjorie's co-worker in a dark alley some night and teach him a lesson. The intensity of his fury shocked Sam, who hated unnecessary violence.

"I'll take care of this for you," Sam said without any real plan in mind. He knew how hard Marjorie worked—the long hours with few free weekends. She'd moved her way up the sales ladder and deserved to be a success. The last thing she needed was someone sabotaging her efforts. The burning desire to protect her seared through him like a surgical laser beam.

"Sam, please. I'm a big girl, I'll find a solution my own way."

"No." He shook his head once, hard. "I want to handle this myself."

"Sam." His reaction wasn't humorous anymore. If she'd known this was the way he was going to be, then she wouldn't have told him about Al. As it was, Marjorie was grateful not to have mentioned the other man's name. "Listen to me. I appreciate your concern, but I don't involve myself in your office affairs—you can't in mine. Things have a way of working themselves out."

"But this heel deserves..."

"Everything he's going to get." She stood and placed her hand on his forearm. "I don't need anyone to rescue me; I've been on my own for a long time now. This guy hasn't made many friends at Dixon's—he won't last long."

"You're sure?" At her nod Sam relaxed somewhat. "Have you eaten yet?"

"No," she answered with a smile, surprised to realize how hungry she was. "Are you offering to feed me?"

"Better than that," he answered with a slow, sensuous grin that edged his strong, well-shaped mouth upward. "I'm willing to cook it for you."

Just looking at Sam made Marjorie feel lightheaded. She could drown in those appealing eyes of his, teddy-bear eyes—dark, deep, penetrating.

"Follow me," Sam instructed, taking her hand and leading her into his kitchen. He was a good cook and thought he might be able to teach her a thing or two.

Sam's kitchen was huge and equipped with every modern convenience. An island with a Jenn Air range top was set up in the middle of the expansive floor. A wide assortment of copper pots, pans and skillets was suspended from the ceiling above the island.

"Wow," Marjorie said, and released a slow, wondering breath. "You must be some chef."

"I try." He pulled out a stool for her to sit on. "First things first." With that he opened the refrigerator where several wine bottles were stored on the top shelf. With little hesitation he drew one out and extracted two tall wineglasses from a cabinet.

Expertly he removed the cork and poured them each a glass, pausing to taste his first. He gave his approval before handing the second glass to Marjorie.

While she sipped her Chablis, Sam placed a huge wok, a large supply of fresh vegetables and a sharp cleaver on the countertop.

It had been hours since she'd last eaten, and the first glass of wine went straight to Marjorie's head. "Here, let me help," she offered, slipping off the top of the stool.

"No, you won't. You're my guest," Sam insisted, noting the way her cheeks were reddening. She was already a little tipsy.

Sam refilled her wineglass, and she took another sip. "So you don't want my help. Have you been talking to my apartment manager?"

"No." Sam chuckled and set about slicing the vegetables in neat, even sections. "This is a recipe a friend of mine from Hong Kong taught me several years back. It's authentic and delicious."

"Is there anything you can't do?" Marjorie asked, only a little intimidated.

"A few things."

She sighed, crossed her legs and sipped some more wine. "My grandmother used to do all the cooking," Marjorie told him.

"Your grandmother?" he prompted. Marjorie rarely talked about her youth.

"Jody and I went to live with her after Mom and Dad were killed in an automobile accident."

"How old were you?"

"Twelve going on twenty. Grandma loved us, don't get me wrong. She tried to make a decent home for the two of us, but she was old and her health wasn't good. The main problem was money. Grandma took care of Jody and the house, and I found work to bring in extra income."

Sam reached for the wine bottle and replenished her glass. The Chablis was loosening her tongue.

"So your grandmother raised you and Jody?"

She nodded, holding the stem of the glass with both hands. "Right. Isn't this room excessively warm?" she asked, and fanned her face.

Suppressing a smile, Sam gazed at her, trying not to laugh outright. "I think I'd better feed you, and the sooner the better."

"I'd rather you kissed me," Marjorie told him, blinked, then covered her mouth with her hand. "Oops, I didn't mean to say that."

Sam pushed the vegetables aside. "Did you mean it?"

Sheepishly she nodded. "I think the wine's gone to my head."

"I think so, too." He walked around to stand directly in front of her. His smile was filled with confident amusement.

Her dark eyes followed his movements and innocently pleaded with him for a kiss. Unable to resist her, Sam leaned forward and gently covered her mouth with his own. His intention had been to appease her until he'd finished stir-frying their dinner, but the instant his lips met hers, he was lost. He deepened the kiss, his lips playing over hers as though she were a rare musical instrument.

His kiss burned through Marjorie like fire raging through dry brush. A low moan rose from deep within her throat. When he reluctantly lifted his head from hers, she swayed, and his hands on her shoulders were all that kept her from tumbling to the floor.

"I think you're right," she admitted. "I need something to eat . . . quick."

Sam's eyes burned into hers, and his strong, steady voice shook slightly. "I was just thinking that we should forget about dinner and continue with the kissing."

She tilted her head up to look into his eyes, resisting the urge to reach out and cling to him. "You were?"

"But you're right."

"I am?" At the moment she didn't think so as she watched Sam turn back to the stove. After a while she stood on shaky feet, unfastened her jacket and removed it. By the time she'd finished loosening the top buttons of her shirt, Sam had their meal ready.

He handed her a plate and pulled a chair up beside her own. The tantalizing scent of hot oil and ginger wafted toward her, and her stomach reacted with a loud growl. Marjorie placed her hand over her abdomen and smiled sheepishly. "Sorry."

"When was the last time you had anything to eat?"

"Noon." Soup. She'd been too upset to down anything else and now she was famished.

Sam used chopsticks, holding the plate with one hand while dexterously using the wooden sticks with the other. Marjorie tried the same thing and nearly dumped her dinner on her lap.

"You'd better use a fork," Sam advised, humor lurking in his eyes as he watched her fumble with the Chinese utensils.

She nodded meekly. Once she had a fork in her hand, she discovered the food was both hot and spicy. Closing her eyes, she savored each mouthful as though she hadn't eaten in weeks instead of hours.

"Oh, Sam, this is really good."

"I do my best," he answered, but his interest wasn't in the dinner. Marjorie, the woman who had tormented his dreams for weeks, was sitting across from him. Part angel, part hellion. Complicated, vital and ripe with such opulent beauty that his blood stirred hotly just sitting close to her. He'd dreamed of having her with him in his home, envisioned carrying her into his room and laying her across his king-size bed. He wanted to love her, ease the ache of loneliness he read in her eyes and make up to her for the childhood she'd lost.

Following the meal, Sam made a fresh pot of coffee. Marjorie poured them each a cup and carried them into the living room. They sat close to each other, and Marjorie tucked her feet up under her and placed her head on Sam's sturdy shoulder.

"You're not going to drift off on me, are you?" he asked gently. His hand curved around her nape, and his fingers stroked the slope of her neck and shoulder.

"If you keep doing that, I will." She felt him smile against her hair. "I'm sorry to be such poor company," she said, uttering the words through a loud yawn.

"You're not."

She half lifted her head. "I don't know what it is, but every time I'm around you all I do is sleep."

"I often have that effect upon women," Sam said, and chuckled. The rich sound of his amusement echoed around the room. He was thinking of going to bed, too, but not in the same sense she was. Holding her close was a tough temptation to handle.

Marjorie tried unsuccessfully to stifle another yawn. "Believe me, I know how women react to you."

"I'd better get you home, kitten."

"Kitten?" No one had ever called her anything but her name, at least not to her face.

"You remind me of one," Sam explained softly. "You're all soft and cuddly."

"I have claws."

Again he smiled. "Now that's something I can personally attest to."

Marjorie was smiling when she unfolded her legs from beneath her and stood. She collected her jacket and purse and paused in the entryway. "It seems I'm always in your debt."

Sam's brow furrowed. "How's that?"

"First you rescue me from the jaws of death..."

"That's a slight exaggeration."

"Then you buy a car from me..."

"One I intended to purchase anyway."

"Next you feed me."

There was a lot more Sam was interested in doing for her, and if she didn't hurry up and leave, he was going to have more problems refusing her.

"Thank you, Sam, once again."

"Thank you, kitten."

They paused in front of the door, and Sam turned her in his arms. His hands locked at the small of her back, pulling her closer against the solid wall of his chest. His hips and thighs pressed against her own, and still they weren't close enough.

Marjorie had no intention of refusing his kiss, not when she craved it herself. His mouth closed possessively over hers, searing his name onto her heart and claiming her soul. Again and again he kissed her with a fierce tenderness, shaping and fitting her lips with his own.

His hands slid down her buttocks in a restless caress, molding her in an intimate embrace. She melted in his crushing hold, sharing his urgency, needing to know that what was happening between them was as real as she'd prayed it would be.

Gently he touched his tongue against the seam of her mouth, coaxing it apart, and when she parted her lips, his tongue slipped inside. Marjorie felt a wild shock surge through her body, and she tightened her hold on his neck, clinging to him for support.

Sam's arms circled her protectively while his tongue explored the soft recesses of her mouth until she shook with a sensation she had never known.

"Sam..."

"Kitten," he murmured. He deepened the kiss, and his hand slid from her back to her midriff and upward to boldly cup her breast and feel the enticing fullness.

Marjorie gasped and her breasts strained against the constricting material of her silk blouse and bra.

Wildly consuming kisses followed, and Marjorie felt as though she were on fire. Never had she felt so willing, so sensuous. There'd been little time for puppy love when Marjorie was in her youth. Later, the men she'd dated had resented her streak of independence. When it came to lovemaking and men, she was shockingly innocent. The sensations Sam had awakened in her had been dormant far too long. Now that she'd discovered love, she wasn't going to let go lightly.

An insistent beeping surrounded them, and Sam's impatient groan told her the noise wasn't the bells on the hill tolling their love.

"What is it?" she whispered, hardly able to find her voice.

"Not what, but who."

She blinked, not understanding.

"That's my pager. I'm needed at the hospital."

Chapter Seven

The phone pealed loudly in the darkened bedroom. At first Marjorie incorporated the irritating sound into her dream. By the third ear-shattering ring she realized it was her telephone.

Without lifting her head from the pillow, she stretched out her arm and groped for the receiver, locating it in time to cut off the fourth ring.

"Yes," she mumbled, and brushed the wild confusion of hair from her face.

"Kitten?"

Marjorie's eyes flew open, and she struggled into a sitting position and reached for the small clock on her nightstand. "Sam?"

"I'm sorry to wake you, but I wanted to be sure you got home safely."

Marjorie blinked and focused her gaze on the illuminated clock dial. It was a few minutes after four. "I didn't have any problems. How did things go at the hospital?"

"Great. Wonderful, in fact."

She relaxed and leaned against the thick goose-down pillow, savoring the warmth that never failed to infuse her whenever Sam called. "Did you deliver another baby?"

"Two actually, or I would have been back hours ago."

"Girls?"

"One of each." Sam felt like a fool calling her at this ungodly hour, but he'd walked into his empty house, and everywhere he looked, he thought of Marjorie. The memory of her presence swirled around him like the soft scent of summer. Often the stark loneliness of his lifestyle had hit him after a nighttime delivery, but never more than it had that evening. He would have given anything in the world to have found Marjorie curled up and sleeping in his bed, waiting for him. Hearing her voice was a poor substitute, but one he couldn't deny himself.

"I realized when I got back to the house," he continued, "that I hadn't asked to see you again." Even to his own ears the excuse sounded lame.

"No, we both had other things on our minds."

"Dinner tonight then?" he asked.

Marjorie wasn't thinking clearly; her mind was clouded with the last dregs of sleep. "What day is this?"

"Friday."

Her disappointment was potent enough to produce a bout of aching frustration. "I can't," she moaned. "My sister is driving up from Portland, and I'm working late both days this weekend."

"I'll take both you and your sister to dinner then." That was an easy enough solution.

"But, Sam..."

"No arguing. Your sister, and anyone else you want, is welcome to join us." He didn't care if he had to buy dinner for every employee at Dixon Motors as long as he could spend time with Marjorie.

"You're sure?"

"Absolutely. And while we're on the subject of dinners and dates, do you have plans for July fourth?"

"No..."

"You don't have to work?"

"No," she murmured, and smiled. "That would be un-American. What makes you ask...about the fourth, I mean?"

"Another doctor and his wife, Bernie and Betty Miller, have a cabin on Hood Canal, and they invited me up. Would you spend the day with me?"

Marjorie closed her eyes to hold back the tears of relief and joy. "I'd consider it an honor."

"I'll let the Millers know then."

They must have talked for another half hour before Marjorie realized that Sam's slow responses revealed his exhaustion.

"Oh, Sam, I'm sorry. You must be dead on your feet, and I'm talking your head off."

Sam's grin was both lazy and content. "No. Listening to you relaxes me. Normally when I get back from the hospital, especially this late, I'm too tense to sleep—too keyed up. Now I feel like I could easily drift off."

"Good night, Sam," Marjorie murmured softly, regretfully. She was falling head over heels for Sam Bretton, knew the pitfalls and still wanted to love him.

"A doctor," Jody squealed with unrestrained delight. The twenty-year-old was a delightful, younger version of Marjorie, the only difference being Jody's hair, which was cut fashionably short, and her more sporty and colorful clothes.

"You behave yourself," Marjorie warned, waving her index finger under her younger sister's nose. Now that her health was back and she didn't have to submit to Jody's orders, Marjorie could more fully appreciate her sibling.

Jody looked her sister full in the eye. "You mean I can't tell Sam about the time you snuck out of the house to kiss Freddy Fletcher behind the toolshed?"

"You do, and I'll box your ears."

The light, musical sound of Jody's laughter filled the cozy apartment. "I have to admit, though, you look a hundred times better than the last time I was here. I wonder if your doctor friend has anything to do with that?"

"I look better because I haven't been forced to down your cooking, which is even worse than my own."

Jody pretended the remark had greatly offended her, but neither had been blessed with talent in the kitchen, and they enjoyed teasing each other.

"So Sam was your physician," Jody said, as she slumped on the couch and crossed her legs Indian style beneath her. "How come you didn't mention him before now?"

"I . . . he . . . well, what really happened is . . ."

"Oh honestly, Marjie, look at your face. You're actually blushing. I can't believe it. My big sister is in love. Well, good grief, it took you long enough."

Embarrassed, Marjorie's hands flew to her cheeks. They did feel hot and were, no doubt, as flushed as Jody claimed.

"You're in love with him, aren't you?" the twenty-year-old asked, pretending to study her nails, but actually aiming her gaze toward her older sister.

"Yes," Marjorie answered honestly.

"Have you gone to bed with him yet?"

"Jody!"

"Well, have you?"

The heat in Marjorie's face intensified a hundred-fold. "Of course not! What kind of question is that?"

Jody's eyebrows rose suggestively. "But you'd like to, wouldn't you."

"I can't believe we're having this conversation." With as much composure as Marjorie could muster, which wasn't much, she reached for her glass of iced tea and took a large swallow.

Amused, Jody pinched her lips together in mock disapproval. "Oh honestly, Marjie, would you stop being my mother long enough to talk to me like a big sister. Tell me everything. I want to know the most intimate desires of your heart."

Despite the subject matter, Marjorie relaxed. "My desires—that's easy."

"Sam?" Jody coaxed.

"Sam," Marjorie repeated. "I can't believe this is happening to me after all these years of being so sensible about men. With Sam everything's different." She paused and then continued, telling her sister how Sam Bretton had stayed with her in the darkest hours following surgery. "I didn't know any man that wonderful existed. I feel giddy every time I'm with him."

Jody nodded knowingly and smiled through a haze of tears.

"Honey, what's wrong?" Marjorie asked quickly.

Using her index fingers, Jody wiped the moisture off the high arch of her cheekbones. "This is the first time that I can remember when you've talked to me like a...sister. You never shared anything with me before—at least not like this. I'm happy for you, Marjie, really happy."

Marjorie blinked back her surprise, ready to argue her point. Then she thought about how right her sister was. She had never felt she could share with Jody; her sister was so much younger that Marjorie didn't feel she could burden Jody with her problems. Jody had to be protected, and because of this their relationship had to be part parent, part sibling—mother, sister, daughter, friend.

"You know something," Jody said, both laughing and crying, her voice unsteady. "I love Sam already."

"Wait until you meet him," Marjorie answered, her own voice wavering. "He's been so good to me."

"You deserve him, Marjie, and he deserves you."

The two sisters wrapped their arms around each other and squeezed tightly, neither willing to let the other go. They had reached a deeper understanding of what it meant to be sisters, and for that Marjorie would always be grateful.

Sam arrived about fifteen minutes later, amazed at Marjorie's sister's warm welcome. He liked Jody immediately but would have appreciated time alone with Marjorie. It seemed a hundred years since he'd last seen her and a thousand since he'd held her sweet warmth against him and relished the special feel of her in his arms.

The evening proved to be a fun one, and he treated the two women to a delicious seafood dinner in a four-star restaurant that overlooked Commencement Bay. Following the meal the three walked along the dock outside the Lobster Shop and gazed at the bright lights that sparkled like shiny stars from the opposite shore.

"I can't remember the last time I ate this well," Jody said, holding her stomach and exhaling a deep, contented sigh. "I'm stuffed."

Marjorie's worried gaze instantly flew to her younger sister. "You're not eating right, and that last comment just said as much."

"I'm in perfect health."

Sam's arm around Marjorie's waist tightened, and she managed to hold back any further argument.

Jody's gaze fell upon the two, and with a smile crowding the corners of her full mouth, she feigned a loud yawn. "I can't believe how tired I am all of a sudden. That drive from Portland can really wear a person out."

Sam and Marjorie shared a secret look and struggled to hide their amusement. Jody couldn't have been any less subtle had she tried.

"I think she's offering us some time alone," Sam whispered close to Marjorie's ear. He was hard-pressed not to flick his tongue over her lobe, knowing her instant response. "Are we going to take it?"

Marjorie's nod was eager.

"Just drop me off at the apartment, and you two can escape," Jody announced, looking pleased with herself. "Far be it from me to block the path of young love."

"Far be it from me to let you," Sam joked, as the three headed toward the restaurant parking lot.

Sam drove directly back to Marjorie's apartment, and Jody hurriedly scooted out of the car, winked and reached for Marjorie's apartment keys. "Don't hurry back on my account."

"We won't," Sam assured the younger Majors. He appreciated what Jody was doing, but he wouldn't keep Marjorie out long. It was obvious the two sisters were close. He's seen for himself the various roles Marjorie played in her sister's life, slipping from one to the other with hardly a breath in between.

Marjorie remained in Sam's car while Jody let herself into the apartment. His hand reached for hers, squeezing gently.

"I like your sister."

"She's impressed with you, too." That was a gross understatement, Marjorie thought to herself. Jody had been giving Marjorie signals all night that showed her wholehearted approval of Sam. The younger girl had elbowed Marjorie twice during the course of the evening. In the ladies' room Jody had gone so far as to suggest that if Marjorie didn't want Sam, she'd take him.

But Marjorie wanted Sam Bretton even more than before. She couldn't look in his direction without her eyes revealing everything that was stored in her heart. She couldn't hide her love for him any longer.

"I have to stop off at the hospital for a minute," Sam said, as he pulled out of the parking lot of Marjorie's apartment complex. "Is that a problem?"

"No, of course not. If you want, I'll stay in the car."

"There's no need for you to do that," Sam came back quickly. "I want to introduce you to a couple of my friends. And this will give you a chance to see the two babies I delivered the other night."

Marjorie's heart shot to her throat. Babies. Sam was as comfortable with them as she was with interest rates

and electromechanically fuel-injected engines. Anyone under the age of two terrorized her; babies made
her nervous and served to remind her of how inadequate she was in the traditional female roles. Her big-
gest fear was that Sam would bring her into the
hospital and expect her to go inside the nursery. He
might even expect her to hold an infant, and then he'd
learn that not only were babies allergic to her, she was
allergic to them!

"How does that sound?" Sam asked, cutting into
her troubled thoughts.

"About the babies?" she hedged.

"Yes, both are..."

"Sam, listen," she said, rushing her words. "Maybe
it would be better if I went back to the apartment with
Jody."

He shot her a puzzled frown. The disappointment
that welled within him was strong. He couldn't understand her hesitation. Sure, she hadn't especially
enjoyed her hospital stay, and he could understand
why. But her hesitation now puzzled him. "Go back
to the apartment? Whatever for?"

Marjorie made the pretense of glancing at her
watch. "It's late and..."

"It's barely after nine," he countered, studying her.
Marjorie was growing more pale by the minute.

Marjorie couldn't look into Sam's eyes and refuse
him anything. "You're right," she said, determination squaring her shoulders. "I'm being silly. Of
course I'll go with you and meet your friends and see
the babies. Everything will be wonderful."

Her voice was falsely cheerful, but Sam decided it was far better for her to confront her fears than leave them unconquered. He'd be with her—nothing would go wrong.

He helped her out of the car and led her into a side entrance and to the elevator beyond. When the door shut, Sam punched the floor number and pulled Marjorie into his arms for a brief, ardent kiss.

Marjorie tried to respond, but her heart was beating as hard and loud as jungle drums, and her insides were quavering with apprehension. She wanted to do everything right with Sam, and her fear of babies was sure to ruin her chances.

Sam pulled her close to his side and stared at the closed doors. Marjorie was his kitten, with her soft, soft skin, her wide, soulful eyes and a heart he longed to fill with his love.

The elevator doors smoothly glided open, and Marjorie braced herself for the inevitable. Sam meant so much to her, and it was vital that she be the kind of woman he needed. Without meaning to, she pressed her flattened palms together and rubbed them back and forth several times. When Sam looked her way, his frown deepening, Marjorie smiled tightly and freed her hands, letting her arms drop lifelessly to her sides.

With his hand at the base of her spine, Sam directed Marjorie into the nurses' station and introduced her to three of the staff members he worked with regularly. The purpose of this visit was more social than anything else. The need to stop in had been partially fabricated in an effort to casually introduce

Marjorie to his peers. It seemed as though she'd been a natural part of his life forever.

"Is Bernie around?" Sam questioned the older nurse, who reminded Marjorie of Bertha Powell. The two could have been sisters.

"Dr. Miller's in the lounge."

Sam reached for Marjorie's hand, lacing her fingers with his own as he led her down the wide hallway.

"Nice to have met you," Marjorie said brightly over her shoulder.

"A pleasure," the older nurse returned. The other two said nothing. Their wide-eyed stares told her that each and every one of them was convinced she wasn't good enough for their beloved Dr. Sam. The feeling persisted long after the staff members were out of sight.

Sam's friend, Bernie Miller, sat at the round table in the middle of the doctors' lounge, holding a Styrofoam cup of coffee. He leaned over the table and held his head up with one hand. When Sam and Marjorie entered the room, he raised his head, his gaze brightening. His fatigued features relaxed into a slow grin.

"Bernie, I'd like you to meet Marjorie Majors."

Slowly Dr. Miller rose to his feet, but his gaze didn't waver from Marjorie's. "Hello, there."

"Hi." She stepped forward and offered him her hand.

"So this is the girl?" Bernie's gaze shot from Marjorie back to Sam as they ended the brief handshake.

"In the flesh." Sam draped his arm across Marjorie's shoulder as he smiled down on her, his gaze filled with warmth. Sam hadn't told many of his friends about Marjorie, but hiding it from his best buddy had been impossible. Bernie had known he'd met someone important the minute Sam casually mentioned her a few days earlier. Bernie had wanted to know all about her, but Sam had hesitated. He hadn't been sure of his own feelings then. Marjorie appealed to him more than anyone in a long time, but there were problems. She wasn't exactly Betty Crocker, and the realization had pulled him up short. Until he'd met Marjorie, the woman he'd pictured in his life had been able to seduce him with her body and whip up a five-course dinner at the same time.

"I understand that you're joining us on Wednesday."

"Yes," Marjorie said, and nodded for emphasis. "Thank you for including me."

Sam poured them each a cup of coffee while she spoke with his friend, then the two joined Bernie at the table. Marjorie mused to herself with glib satisfaction that things were going well. She related well to adults; it was infants and children who caused her to break out in hives.

"I'm going to take Marjorie into the nursery," Sam was saying.

Doing her utmost not to choke on her coffee, Marjorie pushed the cup aside and stood. If she thought her heart had been pounding to a pagan beat in the elevator, now it was crashing like a Chinese gong as she followed Sam out of the doctors' lounge. No doubt the three nurses at the station never had this problem. Any one of them would gladly surrender their eyeteeth to have Dr. Sam Bretton.

He led her down the wide corridor and into the nursery. Rows of bassinets were lined up in uniform fashion. Some of the infants were blanketed in pink, others in blue. Their surnames were written in bold letters in front of their mock cribs. A couple of the nurses that Marjorie had recently met were working with the babies. Both sat in rocking chairs, soothing crying infants.

Sam donned a surgical robe and handed Marjorie one.

"Sam," she whispered, barely able to speak. "There's something you should know."

"Just a minute," he murmured, grinning boyishly. With a gentleness she'd witnessed several times in the last month, Sam lifted a small pink bundle from a crib and looked up at Marjorie, beaming proudly.

"What do you think?" he asked, scooting sideways so she could more easily view the squirming infant in his wide embrace.

Marjorie's eyes dropped to the scrunched-up face and the minute fists as the baby struggled to be free of its bindings. Words nearly stuck in her throat. "He's real cute."

"She, kitten."

"She," Marjorie repeated, her breath coming in shallow gasps.

"Would you care to hold her?"

Her dark eyes rounded with alarm, and she forcefully shook her head. "No...thanks." By the time she'd finished speaking, she'd backed herself out the door.

"Marjorie, are you feeling all right?"

"I'm a little...I'm fine," she managed somehow. "Really."

As carefully as he'd lifted the infant, Sam replaced her in her bassinet. By the time he'd finished, Marjorie was leaning against the wall in the corridor outside the nursery.

"What's wrong?" he asked softly, coming to stand beside her.

"I...it's no big thing."

"You look like you're about to faint."

"Don't worry, I'm not the type," she countered gruffly. "I'm not the kind of woman who goes all mushy at the sight of a baby, either. In case you hadn't noticed, not all of us are alike. There are some of us who cook and crochet and get pregnant at the drop of a hat. And then there are others, like me, who are allergic to baby powder and dirty diapers and content to eat TV dinners the rest of our miserable lives."

Sam's eyes rounded incredulously. "Are you trying to tell me you don't like babies?"

"Sure, I do," she shouted, "in somebody else's arms."

Sam blinked, hardly able to believe his ears. He felt as if the world were crashing in around him. He'd had enough of a problem accepting Marjorie's lack of culinary skills but decided her strength and independence were more important than any domestic qualities. But when it came to having children he wouldn't compromise.

"Babies are fine for the right kind of woman," she cried. Her voice gained in volume with the strength of her convictions. "Unfortunately I'm not one of them."

"You don't mean that." His words were sharp.

By now their heated exchange had attracted the attention of the hospital staff. If Sam's nursing friends had disapproved of her earlier, it was nothing to the censure she felt coming down on her now. Sam deserved someone far more domestic than she would ever be, and every accusing glare said as much.

Without thought for the wisdom of her actions, Marjorie turned and half ran, half walked down the polished corridor to the elevator.

"Marjorie, wait," Sam cried.

She didn't have much choice if she wanted to maintain her dignity. They descended in tense silence. Not even when they left the hospital building or headed toward Sam's car did either speak. By that time Marjorie's throat was so clogged that it felt as though someone had a stranglehold on her. With everything that was in her she yearned to be all Sam wanted in a woman, yet she'd failed miserably.

Sam opened her door for her. His feet felt heavy as he walked around the car and let himself in. He didn't know what to say or how to say it. He wanted a family, longed for children, and he yearned for Marjorie to give them to him.

Marjorie watched him with despair. The tears that had been so close to the surface rained down her cheeks like water over a dam after an early spring thaw, and she turned her head away so he couldn't see. At that moment she would have sold her soul to be different.

Marjorie inhaled a deep, shuddering breath. "You want children, don't you?" He couldn't deny it. Sam Bretton would make a wonderful father; he was a natural. Bill Cosby should take lessons from him.

"Yes." He couldn't make light of his desire for a family. Almost from the beginning he'd pictured Marjorie with a child in her arms—their child. For years he'd been seeking a woman who was strong enough to stand on her own and tender enough to need and love him. These last weeks with Marjorie had led him to believe he'd found that special one . . . until tonight.

"I'm no good with babies, and I'm even worse with children," she whispered in a choked voice. "That's not going to change."

Chapter Eight

For the second time that morning Marjorie checked the picnic basket. Her nerves were shot. She hadn't heard from Sam, nor had she contacted him. For three days she'd done nothing but think about him and how wrong they were for each other. The realization didn't do any good, though; she still loved him, still wanted him, still yearned for them to build a life together. She'd give anything to be the right person for Sam, but she couldn't change what she was, nor could she be someone different.

Now it was the Fourth of July, and she wasn't even sure he'd show up for the picnic and wouldn't blame him if he didn't.

She paused to inhale a calming breath and rubbed her hands down the thighs of her new, frosted-denim jeans. The stiff material had been Jody's idea. Marjorie hadn't told her sister what happened between her and Sam, but Jody had guessed something was drastically wrong. The following morning Jody had insisted they go shopping, claiming there wasn't any ailment a department store couldn't cure. The jeans, Jody claimed, did great things for Marjorie's legs. For all Marjorie cared, they could have been made from sackcloth.

The weather outside wasn't promising; thick gray clouds had formed overhead. As an afterthought she tucked a thick sweater inside the basket.

The doorbell chimed, and Marjorie's heart lurched. She swallowed and opened the door. Sam, dressed in jeans and a striped red T-shirt, stood on the other side. He didn't look any better than she felt. Although he was outwardly composed, turmoil and regret were evident in his eyes and the hard set of his mouth.

He stepped inside her living room and hesitated, then smiled. The movement transformed his face.

"What's wrong?" Marjorie asked, convinced she should never have worn the jeans. So much for Jody's advice. Denim might help her legs, but it didn't do a thing for her hips.

"The jeans," Sam managed.

"They're all wrong, aren't they?" Silently she blamed her sister. Marjorie knew better than to listen to the advice of a college student who was toying with the idea of tinting her hair blue.

"No," Sam murmured.

"I can change, don't worry," Marjorie went on brightly. "It'll only take a minute."

"Don't," Sam said, and smiled briefly. "You look fantastic." His gaze was warm and sincere.

Marjorie thought she would cry. She'd been as taut as a violin bow, as well as nervous and worried. Until the minute he spoke Marjorie had no idea what Sam was thinking. Apparently he'd decided to put the incident in the hospital behind them . . . at least for today. Marjorie knew that they should talk and try to settle this problem, but in three days she hadn't been able to come up with a solution, and from his haggard look, she suspected that Sam hadn't, either. Today they would put their troubles aside and enjoy the holiday. Marjorie was grateful.

"Every woman should look so good in Levi's," Sam murmured again.

A smile curved her mouth. "You honestly like 'em?"

"Yes, kitten, I do."

Sam longed to take her in his arms and hold her, but he dared not touch. These last days without Marjorie had been a self-imposed nightmare. After years of searching for the woman he could love, respect and admire, he'd been convinced he'd found her in Marjorie. No, she wasn't exactly the woman he'd pictured, but he'd discovered he could accept her quirks, loved her all the more because of them. They were part and parcel of Marjorie. But children . . . he'd dedicated his life to reproduction and childbirth. To him children were as essential as food and water. He needed a woman who would willingly give him a family. He could find no compromise on an issue so basic to their lives.

After the night at the hospital Sam had decided to make a clean break from her. There didn't seem to be any purpose in prolonging the agony. Then he'd learned it wasn't that simple. He thought about her constantly, longed to talk to her. After two torturous days he'd known that forgetting about Marjorie would be impossible. He would have to think of something to help him solve this problem.

"I've missed you," he murmured, as his eyes held hers.

"I've missed you, too," she answered, and her voice was weak and filled with regret. "Sam," she whispered, having trouble finding her voice. "I'm so sorry."

"I am, too, kitten." He drew in a deep breath, then exhaled slowly. She couldn't change what she was, and he couldn't help loving her. Dear Lord, he prayed they could find a solution to this, because now that he had found Marjorie, he couldn't let her go.

"Betty," Sam said, his arm loosely draped over Marjorie's shoulder. "This is Marjorie Majors. Marjorie, Betty."

"Hi," Betty Miller greeted cordially, her blue eyes twinkling. She bounced a toddler on her hip, and the shy little boy hid his face against his mother's shoulder. "I'm so pleased you could make it. Can you believe this weather? Only on Puget Sound would we have a fireplace going on the fourth of July."

"Thank you for inviting me."

Betty was slender and pretty, exactly the type Marjorie had always pictured as a doctor's wife. Her deep blue eyes were warm and gentle, and Marjorie doubted that Betty Miller had an enemy in this world.

"The ruffian on my hip is Kevin," Betty added, and encouraged her son to look up long enough to greet their company. Kevin, however, held his fists over his eyes and refused to acknowledge Marjorie or Sam.

"Hi, Kevin," Marjorie offered stiffly but to no avail.

The little boy buried his face deeper into his mother's shoulder. "He's a little bit shy," Betty explained, her face flushed with embarrassment.

"That's all right," Marjorie said, in an effort to reassure her. She understood far better than Betty could realize. Kids instinctively knew she was rotten mother material. Marjorie didn't know how they knew, but they did.

"Kevin, do you want to show Uncle Sam where your daddy is?" Betty asked, and there was a hopeful note in her voice.

To everyone's surprise Kevin nodded eagerly and climbed off his mother's hip. Without looking in Marjorie's direction, the three-year-old held out his hand in order to lead Sam away.

Sam must have noted the distress in Marjorie's eyes, because he murmured something about being right back.

"Take your time," Betty returned. Once Sam and Kevin were out of sight, Bernie's wife let out a soft sigh and changed the topic. "You'd think Bernie had constructed the Empire State Building for the amount of time and effort that's gone into this infamous deck."

The cabin was located on the fertile bank of Hood Canal and was surprisingly modern.

"Bernie built the deck himself?" Marjorie had to admit she was impressed with the wraparound structure off the kitchen. A series of stairs led off the back and onto the sandy, smooth beach below.

"Don't encourage him," Betty warned with a short laugh. "In his former life Bernie claims to have been a carpenter. He thinks he missed his calling." Still grinning, she poured them each a tall glass of iced tea and led Marjorie into the living room. A small fire gave the room a cozy feeling.

Marjorie sat in the overstuffed chair opposite her newfound friend.

Betty's chest rose with a deep breath, and she smiled at Marjorie. "You don't know how relieved I am to finally meet you."

"Me?"

"Sam's talked of little else from the day you went in for surgery."

"He told you about me?" Amazed, Marjorie flattened her hand over her heart.

"In elaborate detail. Does that surprise you?"

"It shocks me." And pleased her. And excited her. Then she remembered there could be no future for them.

"Bernie and I have been waiting years for Sam to finally meet the right woman. We'd almost given up hope. He's so dedicated to his patients. The one thing that's suffered most over the last few years has been his personal life."

"He is a wonderful doctor."

"You won't get any arguments out of me. I know—Sam delivered both Kevin and Shelley."

"Shelley?" There was more than one child?

"Shelley's sleeping, like all good four-month-olds. You'll see her later."

Marjorie only nodded. She liked Betty and didn't want to disillusion Sam's friend with her lack of the mothering instinct.

"Actually I knew Sam before I even met Bernie," Betty explained, gazing into her iced tea. Her face took on a solemn look.

"Are you a nurse?"

Betty nodded. "I know that sounds old hat, but the path of romance was anything but smooth for Bernie and me. It isn't like we viewed each other from across a crowded room and instantly heard fate calling."

"No?"

Betty crossed her legs and grinned sheepishly. "Well, to be honest, I was dating Sam when I met Bernie. Later Bernie was assigned to the ward where I was working."

"So it was being in close proximity that ignited the fires between you?"

Laughing, Betty shook her head. "Hardly. If there were any fires ignited, they were from the arguments we had. Bernie and I couldn't agree on anything, and I found him impossible to work with. Once he even went so far as to warn Sam that I was a meddling busybody and he'd do well not to see me again."

Marjorie found this all a little difficult to believe. She'd been with Bernie and seen for herself the way his gaze softened when he mentioned his wife's name.

"I know it sounds unbelievable now, but we had serious problems." She paused and ran the tips of her fingers over the chair's armrest, caught up in her memories. "It seemed that no matter what I did or how careful I was, I couldn't please the demanding Dr. Miller. Every time he and I were together, we ended up in a shouting match. There wasn't a staff member on the entire floor who would come within twenty feet of us when we got going."

"But what happened to change all that?"

Betty shrugged, then a lazy smile began to grow until it spread to every feature of her round face. "Bernie came to my apartment one night after work. I'll admit he looked terrible, but we'd had another one of our confrontations that day, and I wasn't in any mood to be friendly."

"What did he say?" Marjorie couldn't help being curious.

"He wanted to talk." She paused and grinned. "I told him to take a flying leap into the nearest cow pasture."

Marjorie laughed outright. The idea of tiny Betty standing up to a stern-faced Bernie presented a comical picture. "I don't imagine he was any too pleased with that suggestion."

"No. I could tell he was struggling not to tell me where I should fly. But he didn't. Instead he asked me how serious I was about Sam."

Marjorie suspected that Bernie had been attracted to Betty from the first, but he was decent enough not to get involved with his best friend's girl.

"Now Sam Bretton was a friend," Betty continued, "a good one. We'd dated off and on for years, but there was never anything serious between us. Fun stuff, you know—a baseball game, hikes now and again, that sort of thing. I think the most romantic Sam ever got with me was a peck on the cheek."

"But you let Bernie think otherwise."

"Why not? He'd been a pill from the first. Besides, what was happening between Sam and me wasn't any of his business. I told him that, too."

"I suppose he left then."

"Yeah, how'd you know?"

"Lucky guess," Marjorie said, holding in a knowing smile.

"We didn't argue after that. Not once. Bernie treated me like every other nurse on the ward, and within a week I was so bored I wanted to cry. Until that moment I didn't realize how much I looked forward to sparring with him." She flattened her palm and patted the armrest a couple of times. "That was when Sam entered the picture. He invited me to have coffee with him in the cafeteria after work one day. When I met him, the first thing he did was ask about

Bernie, but unfortunately I didn't have anything to report. Sam looked surprised at that. He claimed Bernie had gotten drunk one night and stormed at him to hurry up and marry me before he—Bernie—did something stupid."

"I can imagine Sam's reaction to that."

Betty grinned and continued. "Sam told him we weren't anything more to each other than friends and he couldn't see the two of us ever getting married."

"What did Bernie have to say to that?"

Betty rolled her eyes toward the ceiling. "Apparently he tried to swing on Sam. You have to understand how out of character that is for Bernie to fully appreciate him doing anything like that."

"I think I can," Marjorie said. Any person who would dedicate his life to the care and well-being of his fellow man would naturally deplore violence. "How did the two of you ever manage to get together?"

"It was easy once I sorted through my feelings. I figured that since he'd come to me once, that I'd have to be the one to approach him. Not right away, mind you. It took some thinking on my part. The most difficult part was realizing I was in love with Bernie Miller and had been for weeks. The hardest thing I've ever done was approach him with an invitation for dinner. Funny thing, though, once we stopped arguing, we discovered how much we had in common. Within a month of our first dinner date we were engaged and— you know the rest of the story."

Marjorie took a sip of her tea. "The two of you are perfect together. It was obvious from the moment I met you that you and Bernie are in love."

"We work on it." Once again she slapped the armrest. "Enough about me. I want to know about you."

"There really isn't much to tell." A bit uneasy, Marjorie spoke in general terms about her job and her sister. The whole time she was talking, she was aware that there was nothing that made her any different than a hundred other women Sam had dated in the past ten years.

"He's crazy about you," Betty commented. "You know that, don't you?"

Marjorie could feel the other woman studying her. Sam might have been crazy for her at one time, but Marjorie had ruined that.

"To be honest, I wondered what made you different. But ten minutes with you and I can understand it. You're exactly the type of woman Sam needs."

Marjorie's look must have revealed her disbelief.

"A doctor needs a woman in his life who has a strong and independent nature. So many other people are constantly making demands on his time and his energy that there's little left for anyone else. Above anything Sam needs a respite from the demands of work. For men like Sam and Bernie death is the enemy, and they'll fight for a life with little or no thought to the physical or emotional cost to themselves."

Marjorie nibbled on the corner of her mouth. "I hadn't thought about it like that." Betty had far more insight into Sam and Bernie's needs than she'd considered. All Marjorie knew was that she loved Sam Bretton and that she would consider herself the most fortunate woman in the world to be his wife.

"I know Bernie so well that I recognize the signs now. He doesn't need to say a word," Betty went on. "There's a look about him, a tiredness in his eyes and in the way he walks. All of those things tell me the kind of day he's had. He'll snap at me every now and again, but I forgive him because I know that he's probably had to tell someone's son or daughter that their mother won't be coming home from the hospital, or he's had to deliver test results that show positive signs of cancer."

The thought of having to give someone such bad news tightened a knot of compassion in Marjorie's stomach.

"The last thing Bernie needs when he gets home is a list of demands from me. I wouldn't do that to him, and you wouldn't do that to Sam. He knows that, just the way I did as soon as we met."

A cool sip of her drink helped alleviate the tightness in Marjorie's throat. "I don't deserve Sam Bretton."

Betty settled back in her chair and grinned sheepishly. "He said almost exactly those same words to Bernie about you."

Marjorie blinked back her surprise and lowered her gaze. Her heart was filled with such misery that it was impossible to hold it all inside. She felt as though she would burst into tears in another minute.

"In fact, Bernie got so sick of hearing about you that he threatened to cancel their poker night if Sam didn't bring you around and introduce you."

"He must have taken him seriously, because we made a trip to the hospital Friday night."

"Bernie mentioned that, too. He told me that one look at the two of you together and he knew Sam had finally found the right woman. By the way, what is it about Sundays with you?"

"Sundays?"

"Yes. Sam phoned the other day and said the only time he can play poker from now on is Sunday afternoons."

Marjorie set the tall glass aside. "I work weekends. Hopefully someday I'll have Sundays free, but that probably won't be for some time yet. Unfortunately."

Slowly Betty shook her head. "Believe me, when a man puts a woman before a long-standing poker game, he's serious about her."

Marjorie dropped her gaze and felt obliged to add, "We aren't serious.... There are problems."

"Wait and see, you'll settle them," Betty returned with unshakable confidence. "Sam's never been more ready for a wife than he is now."

Betty looked as if there were more she wanted to say, but before she could speak the sliding-glass door opened, and the two men plus three-year-old Kevin walked into the house.

"Have you shown Marjorie my deck yet?" Bernie asked, beaming proudly.

Betty tried not to smile and failed. "I hadn't gotten around to it yet."

"I've been thinking that since this project went so well, I might try my hand at something a little more complicated."

Betty eyed her husband speculatively. "Like what?"

"An addition to the house," he said enthusiastically. "I could add on to the master bedroom. You've told me more than once we need more closet space."

"Men," Betty groaned under her breath to Marjorie.

Sam walked over to Marjorie and sat beside her on the cushioned arm of the chair. He slipped his arm around her and cupped her shoulder.

A warm sensation went down into her arm, and when she glanced up, she discovered Sam studying her. The love that sprang into her eyes was as unexpected as it was embarrassing. His fingers bit into her shoulder as his gaze held hers.

"I love you," he whispered. "We'll work this out."

"But, Sam..."

He bent down and kissed the top of her head. "Listen, we'll adopt older kids. Okay?"

Biting into her bottom lip, Marjorie nodded.

Sam reached for her hand, lacing their fingers together, as though bonding them. She loved this man more than she ever thought it was possible to care about another human being. Whatever problems they faced in the future could be conquered with Sam at her side.

"When are we going to eat?" Betty's son demanded, placing his hands on his hips. "I'm hungry." The little boy still wouldn't look directly at Marjorie, but that was an improvement from hiding his face in his mother's shoulder.

"The barbecue's already hot," Bernie told his wife. "I'll put the steaks on now if everything else is ready."

"I want a hamburger."

"And you will get one," his father promised. "Come along, big boy, and you can help your dear ol' dad and Uncle Sam with the cooking."

"Is there anything I can do?" Marjorie volunteered, quickly rising to her feet. "I brought some potato salad and sliced pickles." Sam caught her eye and revealed his surprise. "Deli made," she whispered, and grinning, he nodded.

"Why don't you unpack those while I set the picnic table," Betty suggested.

The room emptied, and Marjorie went over to the wicker basket and lifted the top. The salad was nestled between the pickle jar and the chip dip. As she was drawing it out, she heard a faint cry coming from the back of the house. She paused, then remembered Betty mentioning that the baby had been napping. Marjorie went to the cabinet and proceeded to take out a couple of bowls and fill them with the salad and dip. To her chagrin, the infant's crying grew louder.

A quick check outside told her that Kevin had managed to distract his mother from the job of setting the table and the two were on the beach. Betty was bent over, examining something Kevin was pointing to in the sand. The two men were busy chatting while Bernie stuck T-bone steaks onto the hot grill.

Before Marjorie could call out to either man, the baby's cry split the air.

Alarmed, she ran into the back bedroom. The infant's cries died to a soft gurgle once Marjorie arrived.

"Hi," she said stiffly, standing a good three feet from the crib. "Your mother's on the beach. Would you like me to do something before she gets here?"

The baby's fists flayed the air.

"Don't cry, okay? I'm sure she'll be back any minute." Marjorie raised her hand in an effort to dissuade the youngster.

The infant whimpered softly, and that alone was enough to cause Marjorie to take two steps in retreat. Once four-month-old Shelley realized she was losing her audience, she let go with one loud, earnest cry. She paused then, and inserted her fist into her mouth, sucking on it greedily.

"Oh, I get it," Marjorie murmured, retracing her steps. "You're hungry." She dropped her gaze to her own full breasts. "Hey, sorry, I can't help you in that department." She smiled at her own joke.

The baby gurgled again, seemingly amused by Marjorie's attempt at dry humor.

"I suppose you've got a wet diaper, as well."

Shelley made a chuckling, laughing sound that cut straight through Marjorie's heart. "I don't think I'm going to be much of a help in that area, either. You see, babies and I don't get along."

Shelley Miller giggled at that. Two arms and legs punched the air as she smiled up at the adult leaning over her crib.

Sam came into the house and took a Pepsi from the refrigerator. He looked around for Marjorie, and when he didn't find her, he glanced outside.

Surprised not to see her, he opened the front door, thinking she might have forgotten something in the car. She wasn't there, either. Concerned now, he started for the deck to seek out Betty.

A faint noise stopped him. Almost indiscernible at first, Sam didn't recognize it until he paused and listened intently. The sound was that of a baby cooing happily. Sam turned into the narrow hallway that led to Shelley Miller's bedroom. There he found Marjorie.

She sat in the rocking chair, cuddling Shelley in her arms as though she never intended to let the baby go. Tracks of tears streaked her face, creating a bright sheen upon her flushed cheeks. She sniffled loudly and wasn't able to keep her chin from trembling.

"Marjorie," he murmured, falling to his knees in front of her, hardly able to believe his eyes.

CHAPTER NINE

Sam," Marjorie whimpered softly. "I'm holding a baby."

"I see that, kitten."

"She's so beautiful." A teardrop rolled down her face and slipped from her chin, landing ingloriously on Shelley's cotton jumpsuit. Cooing, the baby reached out to catch the next drop.

With a gentleness Marjorie had come to expect from Sam, he tenderly brushed his hand over her face, wiping away the moisture. "I've never seen a woman as beautiful as you are right this minute."

"Sam, I didn't think I could get close to a baby. I didn't dare dream I'd feel this way—ever."

"I suspected as much," he countered, resisting the urge to wrap her and the baby in his arms and hold them both for eternity. "I prayed it would only be a matter of time until you recognized the mothering instincts were there. They have been all along."

"They're here now," she whispered, smiling and crying at once. "I feel so tender inside—I don't know how to describe it. Sam," she said, raising her eyes to meet his, "if I feel this strongly about a baby I barely know, I can't imagine how much love I'd have for one of my own."

"We'll discover that together, kitten."

The tightness that jammed Marjorie's throat made it impossible to speak. Sam was talking about them having children together, and although the thought frightened her, it thrilled her far more. She yearned to ask him if he meant it and to tell him she was willing, but every time she opened her mouth, all that came out were soft, strangled sounds. She managed to free one hand from beneath Shelley to caress the rugged line of Sam's jaw. Closing her eyes, she pressed her cheek against the side of his head.

Sam edged away from her, and their gazes met and held. The promise between them was more potent than anything Marjorie had ever known. She didn't need words to recognize what was in Sam's heart; his feelings were all there for her to read in his eyes.

Sam bent toward her, and her dark eyes shimmered with an aching need for his love, a need that was echoed in his own heart. Her parted lips offered him an invitation he couldn't ignore.

As her head tilted back, fire seared through her veins. This was the man she loved, the man who had filled her life with purpose and realized her dreams.

He'd helped her to conquer her fears, laying the groundwork to destroy one after another with unlimited patience. He had gently proved to her that there wasn't anything they couldn't face together, nothing the force of their love couldn't overcome.

She gasped and bit into her bottom lip as his mouth explored the exposed hollow of her throat. His fingers moved to her breast, cupping the aching fullness and sending shudders through her body at the exquisite sensations he aroused.

"Oh, Sam," she murmured, not wanting him to stop and knowing he must. "The baby..."

He nodded and gently broke contact, although his hands continued to grip her shoulders. The sight of Marjorie holding Shelley, knowing that someday she would be cradling their own baby, burned through him with the effectiveness of a hot knife. He felt weak with desire, weak and yet so powerful.

"Was that Shelley I heard?" Betty Miller asked, as she came into the small bedroom. If she noticed Marjorie's tears, or the fact that Sam was on the floor beside Marjorie and the baby, she didn't comment. "Thanks for getting her up for me," she said smoothly, and reached for her daughter.

With some reluctance Marjorie surrendered the infant. "She's a wonderful baby."

"I'm convinced Shelley gets that easygoing disposition from her mother," Betty said with a cheerful smile.

Bernie's cough could be heard in the background. "What about her old man?"

"And her father," Betty amended, and shared a secret smile with Marjorie that was a wordless disclaimer.

Marjorie managed to smother a laugh. When she stood, Sam slipped his arm around her waist and gently hugged her. "Do you think it'd be considered impolite to eat and run?" he whispered, so she alone could hear.

"Not if we're not too obvious," Marjorie said after a moment. As much as she liked Bernie and Betty, there were so many things she wanted to tell Sam, so much she yearned to share.

"It's selfish, I know, but I want to be alone with you."

Marjorie wanted it, too, and her gaze told him as much.

"Soon," he promised.

"Soon," she agreed.

By the time they reappeared in the living room, Bernie had finished barbecuing the steaks. They all worked together, and within a few minutes the picnic table on the Millers' newly finished deck was set. The salads, potato chips and other dishes were brought out.

Sam sat beside Marjorie, and the two couples talked and joked throughout the meal. When they'd finished, Marjorie sat on the lounge chair and bounced Shelley on her knee as though she'd been handling babies all her life. Every now and again she felt Sam's loving gaze, and they shared a special look that said more than mere words.

"I can't get over the way Shelley's taken to you," Betty commented, joining Marjorie. The weather had cleared as the lazy afternoon sun burned off the clouds.

"Marjorie's a natural with children," Sam said proudly. "I don't suppose she told you, but Marjorie nearly raised her sister."

"Sam," she cried, embarrassed. "I'm not all that natural."

A sharp shake of his head discounted that notion. "She's been around children most of her life," he added. Studying her, his mouth curved into a faint smile. Sam had prayed that given time, she would recognize most of her fears as unfounded. The mothering instinct was as strong in her as it was in any woman, only Marjorie had failed to recognize it.

Marjorie held out her hand to him, and he gripped it firmly in his own. In many ways Sam understood her better than she did herself. Sometime, somewhere, she'd done something very good in her life to deserve Dr. Sam Bretton.

Late Saturday afternoon Marjorie had dressed and undressed twice, unable to decide what to wear. Sam wanted her to meet his parents. Although Marjorie had readily agreed to dinner with his family, she was a nervous wreck. She'd been in and out of clothes faster than a quick-change artist. Worse, she was convinced that Sam's mother was bound to disapprove of her lack of domestic skills, but Sam himself had dismissed that fear.

Five minutes before Sam was due to arrive, Marjorie chose the floral knit dress Jody had suggested in a frantic phone call Marjorie made to Portland. The outfit was more casual than anything she chose for work, and although she'd sought her sister's advice, Marjorie was doubtful. This meeting was too important, and she longed to make a good impression so as not to embarrass Sam.

She needn't have worried. His parents stepped onto the front porch when Sam pulled into the driveway, and they looked as anxious as Marjorie felt.

"Don't be so nervous," Sam said, reaching over to squeeze her clenched fist. "They're going to love you."

"Oh, Sam, I hope so." She forced herself to relax, uncoiling her fingers and flexing them a couple of times to restore the blood flow. Normally she was able to disguise any uneasiness, but meeting Sam's family had completely unnerved her.

"Mom and Dad have been waiting years to meet you."

"I only hope I'm not a disappointment."

"You won't be, kitten, I promise."

Sam's mother came down the front steps and walked toward the car. Marjorie studied the streaks of silver in the older woman's dark hair, then shifted her gaze to the classic profile. None of the other woman's features resembled Sam's. Not the faint gleam in her dark eyes, not the warm, friendly glow in her complexion. Yet if Marjorie had met her in a crowded room, she would have known instantly that this woman was Sam's mother.

Sam helped Marjorie out of the car and slipped his arm over her shoulders.

"Mom and Dad," she said proudly, "this is Marjorie. Kitten, my parents, Roy and Irene Bretton."

"I hope you don't mind us coming out to greet you like this, but Roy and I couldn't wait another minute." Irene took both of Marjorie's hands in her own and nodded approvingly. "I can't tell you how very pleased we are to meet you—at last."

"Thank you. The pleasure is all mine." She felt stiff and awkward. The inside of her mouth was dry, and yet her hands were moist. Sam's warmth was the only thing that kept the chill of anxiety from seeping all the way through her bones. She had so little to impress this family with—no real background or prestigious relatives. She could offer them nothing but her love for their son.

"Please come inside. Dinner's almost ready," Irene invited, leading the way. "I fixed your favorite, Sam—fried chicken, potatoes and gravy with my homemade biscuits."

"Mom's a wonderful cook," Sam explained, grinning down at her. He hoped Marjorie knew that he wasn't concerned about her penchant for burning water.

Marjorie's return smile was feeble at best.

"I'll give Marjorie all your favorite recipes if she wants them," Irene offered.

Marjorie nodded eagerly, knowing it would be a complete waste of time, but she hated to disillusion Sam's mother so quickly. Later she would explain that her presence in the kitchen invariably resulted in a fiasco. When she turned on the stove, the entire Tacoma Fire Department went on standby.

"I better go check on the chicken," Sam's mother murmured, as soon as they entered the house.

The luscious smells that greeted Marjorie could rival a four-star restaurant. It was obvious that Sam had underplayed his mother's culinary abilities.

"Let me help," Marjorie offered hurriedly.

"Nonsense, you're our guest." Irene gestured toward the sofa. "Sit down and make yourself at home. I insist."

Marjorie smiled and tried to relax. Sam's parents were exactly as she'd expected—warm and sincere.

She lowered herself onto the wide sofa. An afghan, crocheted in the fall colors of gold, orange and brown, was spread across the back.

Sam claimed the seat next to her and reached for her hand. His father saw the gesture and grinned proudly, as though he were personally responsible for bringing the two of them together.

Within a couple of moments Irene Bretton had returned. "Dinner will be ready in another fifteen minutes," she announced, and took the chair beside Sam's father.

Roy Bretton looked all the more pleased. "Good. We have enough time for a cocktail." He eyed his son intently as though he expected Sam to make some momentous proclamation.

"Dad collects bottles from several local vineyards," Sam explained, ignoring his father's look.

"There are a dozen or so excellent wines bottled right here in Washington state," Roy added, filling in the conversation. "I found another superior winery recently, near Bonney Lake."

"That's close to Buckley," Sam added for Marjorie's benefit. Both Buckley and Bonney Lake were suburbs of Tacoma.

She nodded and started to relax against the back of the sofa. There wasn't anything to be nervous about, especially since Sam's parents appeared more anxious than she.

"Give me a hand, son," Roy said, standing. "I'll let you choose what bottle we should open."

"Sure."

The two men left the room, leaving Marjorie and Irene alone.

"Sam has spoken fondly of you on several occasions," his mother said, clearly seeking a way to start the conversation. "His father and I are very proud of him."

"You have every right to be."

"It'll take a special woman to share his life."

Marjorie dropped her lashes, fearing that Sam's mother was suggesting that she wasn't the right one for their only son. Her heart pounded wildly, filled with doubts.

"I knew from the moment he mentioned your name that you were special to him." She smiled and smoothed her hand across her skirt in a nervous gesture. "A mother knows these things about her children. For instance, I knew long before Sam did—or even his father did—that our son would be a physician. Roy was sure Sam's interest involved animals. He had several pets and was forever collecting more."

"He's the kindest, most generous man I've ever known."

"His nature always was generous," Irene went on to say. "That boy brought home more stray dogs than the city pound ever collected. His heart would melt over things that you and I would hardly notice." She warmed to her subject and scooted forward in the chair, her face bright with love for Sam. "I remember one time—he must have been around ten or twelve—anyway, he found an orphaned kitten in a rainstorm—a sickly, weak, half-drowned cat. By the time he got her home, the poor thing was more dead than alive."

Marjorie's smile went weak. Sam called her kitten, had for weeks now, and like the stray cat he'd found in his youth, she, too, was an orphan. Little things played back in her mind. Minor incidents cleared as they came into focus. Puzzle pieces fell into place, painting a bold picture. Sam was a rescuer, always had been and always would be. He'd seen it as his duty to take care of her as she was orphaned and frightened the night she went into surgery.

When they'd first started dating each other, Sam had tried several times to rescue her. He'd wanted to step in when Al had cheated her out of her sales commission. He'd bought the Mercedes more for her benefit than his own. Now that she was seeing him regularly, she knew that he had a perfectly serviceable automobile and had no reason to purchase another.

"What happened with the kitten?" Marjorie inquired, almost afraid to ask.

"He nursed her back to health. You should have seen that silly cat. She was the most prickly, bad-tempered thing—wouldn't let anyone near her. You'd think she would have been more appreciative of everything Sam had done for her."

The knot in Marjorie's stomach tightened to a punishing level of discomfort. After her surgery she'd lashed out at Sam at every turn. At one point when he had refused to release her from the hospital when she felt it was time, she'd accused him of getting a kickback from the staff. Later she'd felt guilty for being so short-tempered and had apologized.

"He... Sam kept the... cat, though?" she asked, already knowing the answer.

"Named her Kitten and ignored her bad moods."

"Did he lose interest after a while?" Here, too, Marjorie knew the answer.

Irene nodded. "It was bound to happen. Summer came and Sam had his friends. He kept Kitten for a pet, and she became a regular member of the family. I remember the funniest thing about that cat. The first time Kitten became a mother, she wouldn't let anyone

close to her except Sam. She mewed and purred, and
it was Sam who was with her when she gave birth to
her litter. Years later when she died, Sam was in his
first year of high school, I believe... and he was real
broken up for a long time afterward. But he got over
her and has owned several cats since.''

Marjorie struggled to disguise her distress. All his
talk about accepting her as she was, loving her and
needing her was a lie. All lies. Sam hadn't accepted
her. He never had. She was a pitiful, lost soul, helpless and in need of being rescued. From what his
mother told her and from what she'd seen herself,
Marjorie was forced to admit that Sam had yet to accept how truly independent she was. And like the kitten from his youth, Sam would replace her, too. His
interest would wander, and his feelings for her would
change. She would easily be replaced just as the orig-
inal kitten had been.

A numb, tingling sensation spread to her arms and
legs, leaving her paralyzed. She felt physically ill and
emotionally distraught.

How she made it through the dinner was a mystery
to her. Somehow she managed to say and do what was
expected of her as though nothing were wrong. She
answered his parents' questions and responded ap-
propriately to what was going on around her. Yet the
world was crashing down around her feet.

At one point she remembered Sam's father com-
menting that she didn't eat enough to keep a bird alive
and Sam's response. He claimed that he planned on
taking care of her from now on. It had taken every

ounce of composure Marjorie possessed not to inform him that she was perfectly capable of taking care of herself. She didn't need him to see to her meals or that she made enough money to pay the rent or anything else.

By the time they left Marjorie had never been so grateful to get away from anywhere in her life. The sun had set, and dusk had settled over the landscape. Grateful for the cover of night, she hoped that Sam wouldn't notice how pale she was or how sick to her stomach she felt.

Neither spoke as they rode back to her apartment, and when they arrived, Sam climbed out of the car and walked her to her door.

"Invite me inside," he said.

Marjorie felt so unsure, so unsettled. She nodded and unlocked the front door. "I'll make coffee," she murmured, heading toward the kitchen.

Sam followed her. She'd been unusually quiet, but then so had he. All evening he'd been mentally rehearsing everything he wanted to say to her. It wasn't every day a man asked a woman to be his wife, and he wanted to make this moment special.

Briefly he toyed with the idea of pulling the diamond out of his pocket and just handing it to her. But that seemed so abrupt, especially when there was so much he longed to tell her. First he planned on saying how loving her had changed his life. Since he'd met Marjorie, he felt totally alive. He loved her—that much was obvious—and had cared about her for weeks, but telling Marjorie that he loved her was too inadequate, especially since there was so much more to it than mere words.

Marjorie's hands shook as she turned on the faucet to fill the teakettle. Her back was to him when she stood in front of the sink and spoke.

"I like your parents."

"They like you, too, kitten. I knew they would."

She flinched. "Why do you call me that?"

"Kitten?"

Nodding, she set the kettle on the stove.

"I'm not exactly sure," Sam responded. "I had a cat named that once."

"The one you found in a rainstorm?"

He glanced up, surprised. "Yes. How'd you know?"

"Your mother mentioned it." She swallowed tightly, still unable to turn and face him. "She told me what a prickly, ungrateful cat she was."

Sam chuckled. "She came around in time."

"Like I did," Marjorie said in a wobbly but controlled voice.

"You?" Sam asked, surprised. "I thought we were talking about Kitten."

"We are!" She whirled around to face him, her hands braced against the counter. "Me. I'm Kitten."

Sam looked stunned. "That's ridiculous!"

"Tell me, Sam, why did you buy the Mercedes? You didn't need another car."

He shifted uncomfortably. "No, I had the Buick, but it's a couple of years old now and . . ."

"And you wanted me to collect the commission from the sale."

"All right," he said, struggling not to respond to the anger in her voice. "That's true, but I was looking for a way to see you again, and buying the car seemed a perfect solution."

"It was an expensive one, don't you think?"

"I didn't care."

"This may surprise you, Sam Bretton, but I care. In fact, I care a great deal. I don't want your charity. The next time you want to throw money away, give it to the Cancer Society."

"It wasn't charity," he shouted.

Marjorie ignored that, clenching her hands into tight fists at her sides. "What was it about me that attracted you in the first place?" She didn't give him a chance to respond. "There's nothing that makes me any different than a thousand other women who parade through your office."

Drawing in a calming breath, Sam waited a moment before answering. "This conversation isn't getting us anywhere. I suggest..."

"You can't answer me, can you, Sam?"

"I think it would be best if I left and gave you a chance to calm down."

"I don't need any time," she shouted, and to her horror her voice cracked.

Unable to see her cry and not do something to ease the pain, Sam took a step toward her and held out his arms. "Kitten, listen..."

"Don't call me that," she cried, pointing her index finger at his chest and retreating several steps. "Or I'll...I'll..." She couldn't think of anything to threaten him with. "Or I'll scream," she said finally.

"Or worse yet, you might cook for me."

Marjorie's eyes widened with the pain his words inflicted. "Just leave, Sam. The next time I need someone to rescue me, I'll give you a call. But don't wait around for me to phone. It might astonish you to learn that I'm a capable human being."

His frustration was nearly overwhelming, and Sam paused to rub his hand along the back of his neck. "I didn't mean that wisecrack about your cooking."

Her back stiffened with resolve. "I meant every word I said," she responded coolly, struggling to maintain her crumbling composure.

"No, you don't. You love me."

He was so confident, so sure of himself that Marjorie wanted to kick herself for being so gullible. The signs had been there from the beginning, and she'd refused to see them, refused to believe them. Her love for Sam had blinded her from the truth. She was a charity case to him in the same way the kitten had been all those years ago. He may believe he felt something for her now, but time would prove him wrong. He honestly believed she couldn't get by without him.

"Marjorie, I'm not exactly sure what's going on in that twisted mind of yours, but if you want me to tell you that I associated you with the lost kitten, then I'll admit as much—but only at first."

The room swayed, and she reached out a hand in an effort to maintain her balance. Briefly she closed her eyes. "You admit it?"

"But that was only in the beginning," he added softly. "You were so fragile, so afraid, and there was no one there for you when you were ill."

"Do I hear violin music in the background?" Marjorie taunted. It dented her considerable pride to hear Sam refer to her in those terms. She trembled. To be fair, she remembered how she'd clung to him, begging him to stay with her. That had been a low point in her life, and now he was using it against her. Worse, he hadn't an inkling of why she was so offended, and she'd thought he knew her so well.

"Later I was attracted to your courage," he added, ignoring her gibe. "And your pride and your candor. I discovered that I spent half my life thinking about you. When you were discharged, I racked my brain for days trying to think of a way to see you again. I wanted to help you—and I finally came up with the idea about buying the car. By then I knew you were special."

"As I explained before, I don't need your charity donations."

"It wasn't charity in the way you think," Sam shouted, losing his patience. "Damn it, Marjorie, the only thing I did was help you, and you make it sound like I've committed some terrible crime.''

As far as Marjorie was concerned, he had.

''I was in love with you then—only I didn't know it. I love you now. More than I thought it was possible to love another human being. If you don't want me to call you *kitten* again, then fine, I won't.''

A tense silence wrapped itself around them. Marjorie couldn't believe that she would have the most important discussion of her life while standing in her kitchen waiting for a kettle to boil.

Sam's level gaze crossed the width of the room to trap hers. His anger had vanished as quickly as it had come, leaving his face an impassive mask of pride. Abruptly, he pivoted away, his impatient strides carrying him to the door. He paused and turned toward her.

''There's a diamond ring in my pocket, Marjorie. I'd planned to ask you to be my wife.''

Calmly she met his gaze. She wanted Sam. The temptation to swallow her doubts and dismiss her pride nearly overwhelmed her. She would have, too, if she hadn't remembered what his mother had said about Sam losing interest in the kitten after a while. He had his friends, his mother had said. There was nothing to guarantee that anything would be different for Marjorie, and within a few months he'd regret having married her.

"I think you already know my answer to that," she said, looking everywhere but at the huge diamond he now held in his hand.

"You're right—I do know." With that, he inserted the ring back inside his pocket. Then he turned and walked away from her in lightning-quick strides.

The door slammed, and feeling incredibly weak, Marjorie cupped her hand over her mouth and leaned against the counter.

Chapter Ten

Confounded, Marjorie stepped out of her manager's office and paused, her hand lingering on the doorknob. Her mind was racing with the details of her conversation with Bud, the dealership's sales manager.

"Well, what happened?" Lydia wanted to know. She walked around the customer-service counter and stood expectantly in front of her friend. When Marjorie didn't immediately respond, Lydia waved her hand in front of Marjorie's bemused face.

The action captured Marjorie's attention. "I got a promotion," she said, shaking her head, still befuddled. Starting the first of the month her Sundays would be free. For weeks her schedule had conflicted with Sam's. Now, when it didn't matter if she had the day off, her Sundays were open. Life was filled with such ironies.

"A promotion!" Lydia cried. "Hot dog!"

"I can't believe it myself," Marjorie returned, and lightly shook her head in an attempt to dispel her pensive mood. She'd been numb for days; nothing seemed to penetrate the dull ache that had ruled her thoughts and actions since she'd last seen Sam. Not even this promotion, which would have given her plenty of reason to celebrate a week earlier, had sunk into her consciousness.

"What did Bud say to Al Swanson?" Lydia asked next, her eyes round with curiosity.

"I'm not sure... he's still in there." Marjorie had noted how disgruntled he'd looked when Bud announced her promotion. That alone had been worth the apprehension she'd suffered all morning before the meeting.

"And you thought you were going to get fired." Lydia flashed her a triumphant smile and shook her head knowingly. "What did I tell you?"

"Not to worry," Marjorie quoted back to her friend in a monotone, and rolled her eyes toward the ceiling.

Lydia was obviously pleased that her words had proven to be prophetic. "Now all I have to do is straighten out this mess between you and Dr. Sam."

Marjorie stiffened at the mention of his name. "Don't even try," she said forcefully. "As far as I'm concerned, the subject of Sam Bretton is off-limits."

"What did he do, for heaven's sake?"

"Lydia, I already told you, I refuse to discuss the matter!" Purposeful strides carried her across the showroom floor. Once again she was running away, doing anything she could to escape the emotional pain that came when anyone asked her about her doctor friend. Before she'd met Sam, Marjorie had prided herself on her ability to confront unpleasantness. Since her last evening with Sam, she found it easier to hide than deal with her feelings.

Undeterred, Lydia followed her friend. "Hey, we're talking about the man who had you waltzing around here with your head in the clouds not more than a week ago. Something happened, and I want to know what it was!"

"Lydia, please, just drop it." The pain was so fresh that even hearing someone casually talk about Sam produced an ache that came all the way from her soul. Marjorie walked into her office and braced her hands against the side of her desk, inhaling deeply, praying the action would alleviate the surge of emotional pain. She'd done a great deal of thinking since the last time she'd seen Sam. As much as she hated to admit it, she needed him. The realization that she depended on him hadn't been easy to swallow. She loved Sam, but she hated to think she was the subject of his charity.

Following close on Marjorie's heels, Lydia came into the office and shut the door. "Listen, I've tried to be a good friend—"

"I know," Marjorie said, cutting her off, "and I appreciate that, but there are some things that are better left alone." She couldn't deal with Lydia's questions and answer her own. She whirled around to confront her co-worker. "And this is one of them."

Lydia hesitated, shrugged her shoulders and pinched her mouth into a tight line that revealed her displeasure. "But if you'd just tell me what he did that was so terrible, then I could hate him, too."

Marjorie could deal with any multitude of problems—irate customers, unreasonable loan officers, cheating salesmen—but her friend's persistent inquisitiveness wore her down.

She crossed her arms over her chest and exhaled a slow, laborious breath. "Sam called me *kitten*."

Before she could add more, Lydia's mouth fell open in astonished disbelief. "That was it?"

"No. He asked me to marry him, too."

A pregnant pause followed as Lydia's eyes narrowed in speculative scorn. "You're right," her co-worker said in mock disgust. "The man should be sent before a firing squad. He wanted to marry you—well, of all the nerve!"

All Marjorie could manage was a sharp nod.

Lydia ran her fingertips over the top of the desk, avoiding eye contact. "Marjorie...when was the last time you had a decent vacation?"

"About ten years ago. Listen, I can see what you're getting at. You think I've gone off the deep end, and maybe I have. I don't know anymore. I...turned Sam down—my reasons are my own. Just accept that I know what I'm doing, and it's for the best, and kindly leave it at that."

"I can't believe you turned Dr. Sam down!" Lydia glared at her as though Marjorie should be psychoanalyzed that very minute. "The most marvelous man I've ever known, and he wanted to marry you and..."

"And I refused him," Marjorie said flatly.

"You're not seeing him again?"

"No...I don't think so."

"And that's the way you want it?" The incredulousness was back in Lydia's voice, raising it half an octave.

Marjorie couldn't answer yes. Lying to Lydia was one thing, and trying to fool herself was another. She was slowly shriveling up without Sam. Her days felt like empty, wasted years. The hours dragged, especially when she was home alone. The walls seemed to close in around her, suffocating her. Normally Marjorie enjoyed her own company, but since she'd been without Sam, even the everyday routines seemed useless. The happy expectancy was missing from her life, as was the excitement. Without Sam, her future looked astonishingly bleak.

It would have been far better, Marjorie decided, if she'd never met the good doctor. Again and again she'd gone over the events of that last evening with his family looking for some misunderstanding, seeking a solution that would salvage both their prides. But Sam had made that impossible. He'd admitted openly that he pitied her, and she was scared to death of needing him. What a mess this had turned out to be!

Lydia's steady gaze lacked any sign of sympathy. "It's your decision."

Marjorie's gaze held her friend's. "I know."

Her co-worker headed out of the office. "Be miserable then. See if I care."

With Lydia gone, the emptiness inside her small office was oppressive. Dejected, Marjorie sat at her desk and read over some paperwork she'd been putting off. However, nothing held her attention for long, and within moments she was silently staring at the walls, her thoughts focused on Sam.

A minute later Lydia burst into her office and excitedly clapped her hands. She slouched forward and marched around Marjorie's desk in a slow, Indian war dance.

"Lydia! What's going on?"

"Oh Lordy, I love this."

Sam. Marjorie's heart rocketed into space. He'd come for her. He'd decided that his life would be an empty wasteland without her. He'd realized he honestly needed her.

"Sam?" Marjorie asked expectantly, half rising out of her chair. "He's here?" Oh, please, God, she prayed, let him be here.

"Sam? Heavens no." Lydia gave her an odd look and shook her head. "It's Al Swanson. Bud just gave him the ax."

"Bud fired Al Swanson. You mean he's leaving?"

"From the way he's packing up his things, I'd say he couldn't wait to get out of here. He'll be gone in five minutes."

"Oh." Marjorie experienced little elation at the news. A week before her behavior would have rivaled her friend's. Now all she felt was a cloying sense of disappointment that Sam hadn't come for her. Discouraged, she reclaimed her seat.

"Apparently," Lydia went on to explain, "one of Al's fake deals backfired on him. Bud found out about it, and Al's out of here." She jerked her thumb toward the front door.

Marjorie had known from the first that Al was his own worst enemy, and once given enough rope, he'd do himself in without any help from anyone else.

Crossing her arms, a subdued Lydia paused to study her friend. "You thought Sam had come to talk to you?"

Marjorie's fingers tightened around the pencil she was holding; it was a miracle it didn't snap in two. "It wouldn't have done any good."

"Hey, he could have withdrawn his marriage proposal. That might have settled things, don't you think?"

Marjorie shook her head. "Lydia, please. I don't want to talk about him."

"Hurt too much?" her friend asked, lowering her voice into a soft, coaxing tone.

The answer was all too obvious and didn't require a response. Marjorie was lost without Sam, but she would get over him in time. The only question that remained was how long it would take. A lifetime, her heart told her, but Marjorie refused to listen.

Two days later, a cocky smile curving her lips, Lydia sauntered into Marjorie's office, her hands clasped behind her back.

Pretending she'd been interrupted, Marjorie glanced up from the report she was reading. "You look like the cat that just swallowed the canary."

"Really?" Lydia swayed back and forth on the balls of her feet. "I have a tasty tidbit of information, if you're interested."

"About Al Swanson?" The details of what had happened between the salesman and the manager had been the favorite topic of conversation with the other staff members all week. The rumors had been flying around the dealership like combat planes, dropping bombs of speculation.

Lydia shook her head. "What I have to tell you involves a certain doctor, but according to you I'm not supposed to mention his name."

"Sam?" Marjorie's heart stopped, then pounded frantically against her ribs.

"The one and only."

The temptation to strangle Lydia was powerful. Marjorie returned her gaze to the report she'd been studying. "I refuse to play your games, Lydia."

"Okay," she announced with typical nonchalance. "If you don't care, then far be it from me to announce that the very doctor in question happens to be in this building at this precise minute."

Marjorie's gaze froze. "Here?"

"Not more than twenty yards from this office door, if you must know."

The papers Marjorie had been holding slipped from her fingers and fell to the top of her desk. Uncaring, she left the scattered sheets there.

"But you apparently are over Dr. Sam," Lydia commented, studying the ends of her polished nails, "so it would be best if you stayed holed up in here and did your best to pretend he isn't anywhere around."

Without realizing what she was doing, Marjorie stood, her knees barely strong enough to keep her upright.

"I don't mind telling you," Lydia said, grinning, "I'm having a difficult time not giving Dr. Sam a piece of my mind. The man is obviously a pervert!"

Marjorie blinked, sure she'd misunderstood her friend. "Sam's nothing of the sort."

"Imagine Dr. Sam wanting to get married," Lydia continued with a sigh. "Doesn't he realize how old-fashioned that is? A woman should live with a man fifty, maybe sixty years before making that kind of commitment. Dr. Sam expects too much."

As best she could, Marjorie ignored her friend's sarcasm. "Sam's here?"

Smiling unabashedly, Lydia nodded. "You'll see him the minute you walk out of this office."

Nothing could have kept Marjorie where she was.

As Lydia had claimed, Sam was in the dealership, standing at the service counter. For a solid minute Marjorie was unable to breathe. He looked tired, overworked, hassled. He wasn't taking care of himself, and he looked as though he'd lost weight. As if drawn by a magnet, Marjorie walked to his side.

"Sam." His name came from her lips without her even being aware she'd spoken out loud.

He tossed a look over his shoulder and froze when his eyes held hers.

"Hello," she said in an effort to avoid calling attention to herself. "How are you?"

"Fine," he answered stiffly. "And you?"

"Okay...wonderful, actually."

"Yeah, me, too."

A tense silence followed while Marjorie struggled for something more to say. Her gaze fell to the service desk. "Is something wrong with the car?"

He shook his head. "It's time for an oil change."

She nodded.

The taut quiet returned.

"...babies?"

"...car sales?"

They spoke simultaneously.

Sam gestured with his hand. "You first."

"I got a promotion." She didn't mention that her Sundays would be free from now on; she couldn't see the point.

"Congratulations."

She attempted a smile. "Thank you." In the ensuing silence Marjorie motioned toward him, indicating it was his turn. "You look like you've been busy."

He nodded. "I delivered another set of twins last week."

"Girls?"

"No, both boys. Identical."

"Oh." For the life of her, Marjorie couldn't think of another thing to say. Small talk had always been her forte, and there were a thousand other things she wanted to tell him, but couldn't.

Seeing him like this made her feel so unsure, so uncertain. Her mind stumbled over her thoughts. Kitten wasn't such a terrible name, she realized. So she'd reminded him of a half-drowned cat; no doubt that was the way she'd looked when she visited his office that first time. She loved the way his pet name for her sounded on his lips, almost as though the word were a gentle caress. So she needed him. That wasn't such a terrible thing. It was time—more than time—that she faced the fact that needing someone was normal and right. It was on the tip of her tongue to tell him so when Bud, Marjorie's manager, strolled past.

"There's a customer here to see you."

Feeling guilty, although she didn't know why, Marjorie nodded and glanced over her shoulder. "I guess I'd better get back to work."

Sam didn't respond. "I suppose you should."

"Goodbye, Sam."

"Goodbye, kitten." The instant the word slipped out of his mouth, Sam wanted to take it back. "I apologize. I didn't mean to say that."

"Don't worry. Kitten's not such a bad name."

"Only it's not right for you," he said with open defiance, his gaze hardening.

Marjorie wasn't in any position to argue with him; holding back tears required all the energy she could muster. "Right," she answered weakly. "It isn't for me."

Without looking back, Marjorie moved outside where the insurance salesman she'd talked to earlier in the week was waiting for her. As she walked out the door, she heard Sam ask what time he could expect his car to be finished. By the time she returned, he was gone.

Lydia seemed to be waiting for her when Marjorie came back into the dealership. Her friend walked around the customer-service counter and came over to meet her. "Well, what did he have to say?"

"The insurance salesman?" she asked, playing stupid.

"Of course not. I want to know about Sam!"

"Nothing happened."

"But he must have said something! You two talked for a full ten minutes. I timed you. You must have gotten something settled in that amount of time."

"Unfortunately we didn't."

"But, Marjorie, this craziness had got to stop. I talked to Mary, Dr. Sam's receptionist, and she told me he hasn't been the same from the moment you two split. He's melancholy and moody, and everyone knows that's not the least bit like him."

"He'll get over it," she said flippantly.

"Yes," Lydia returned with barely controlled anger. "But will you?"

Her co-worker's words echoed in her mind for the remainder of the afternoon. Lydia was right. Her world was crumbling at her feet, and she was too

proud, too stubborn to do something about it. Just
seeing Sam again had proven that. She was ruining her
life over something incredibly silly. She'd overreacted
and behaved stupidly, and the time had come to own
up to that.

Filled with determination, Marjorie marched over
to the service department.

"What time did you tell Dr. Bretton his car would
be ready?"

Pete, the mechanic who had been with Dixon
Motors for ten years, flipped the pages of the service
order. "After three. As I recall, he told me he wouldn't
be in until six."

Marjorie nodded, pleased. "Have you finished with
the car?"

"Yeah. It seemed pointless to change the oil on a
vehicle that doesn't even have a thousand miles on it.
But we did it—couldn't see the point in arguing with
him."

That small bit of information sent Marjorie's spir-
its soaring. Sam must have used the Mercedes as an
excuse to see her. Her relief felt like a thirst-quenching
rain after a long August drought. "Could I have his
keys, please?"

The mechanic gave her an odd look. "You want Dr.
Bretton's car keys?"

"Right. When he comes in, send him to my office."

The barrel-chested mechanic scratched the side of
his head. "If that's the way you want it, Ms. Majors."

"I do. Thanks, Pete."

The remainder of the afternoon crept by. At precisely six Marjorie was waiting in her office. Sam didn't keep her in suspense long.

He knocked once and stepped inside. "What's this about you having my car keys?" he demanded, short-tempered. He'd been a fool to think that coming to the car dealership would solve anything with Marjorie. She wanted blood, and he wasn't about to give it to her. The more he reviewed their earlier conversation, the angrier he became. That wounded, hurt look had been in her eyes, as though he'd greatly wronged her. All he'd ever wanted was to marry her and make her happy, and she'd reacted as though he'd insulted her.

Marjorie blinked. "Yes, I have your keys."

Sam held out his open palm. "I'd like them back."

"Of course." She remained outwardly calm, but adrenaline was racing through her system as though she were running the Boston marathon. "I have a couple of questions first, if you don't mind answering them."

Sam made a show of glancing at his watch. "Make it quick—I have an appointment."

"Oh, Sam, you always were such a poor liar."

He snapped his jaw closed and pulled out a chair. "As it happens, I do have to be someplace in less than an hour. But obviously my word isn't to be trusted."

"This will only take a minute."

He crossed his legs, hoping to give the impression of indifference. Nothing could be farther from the truth. Anger was his only defense against Marjorie. It was either yell at her or yank her into his arms and kiss some sense into her.

Her fingers closed around the cold, metal keys. "It's about that ring you offered me."

Sam shot to his feet. "Listen, Marjorie, I'm not upping the ante in this marriage business. We're talking about our lives here, not a car deal. There are no counteroffers."

"Yes, I know."

"The offer stands as it was."

"All right," she said, her voice strong and sure.

"All right, what?"

"I'll marry you."

If Sam had been flustered before, it was nothing compared to the confusion he felt now. "You will?"

"That is . . . if you still want me for your wife."

He ran his splayed fingers through his hair. "What happened? Did you check around and discover that you could make a better deal with me?"

"No...that's not it at all." This was going so much worse than she'd hoped.

He eyed her speculatively. "I'll call you *kitten* any time I damn well please!"

She nodded, because speaking would have been impossible.

"We won't have a long engagement, either. I want us married before the end of the summer."

She met his fiery gaze with feigned calm, then answered him with a quick nod of her head.

He mellowed somewhat and lowered his voice. "Do you have to check this out with your manager?"

"No."

His gaze moved to the shimmering moistness of her lips. He was dying to hold her, starved for a taste of her, and just looking at her disturbed his concentration. His control was slipping fast. Walking around to her side of the desk, he reached for her. Hungrily his mouth devoured hers as he pulled her hard against the solid length of his body so she'd know how desperate he'd been without her. His hand roamed possessively over her, molding her to him, uncaring that anyone outside the office might be watching.

Only partially satisfied, Sam dragged his mouth from her, his hunger sated for the moment.

The iron band of his arms held her a willing prisoner. "Sam, I love you...I'm sorry to be so insecure. I don't know what made me say those things. It's just that I've been on my own so long that it hurt my pride to think you pitied me and I..."

"It doesn't matter, kitten," he said, his voice husky and thick against her hair.

Overcome by a searing happiness, she laughed breathlessly. The sound was short and sweet. "I can't imagine why I objected so strongly when I love the name *kitten*."

"Good, because I meant what I said about calling you that."

Her arms circled his waist and her heart swelled. She was home, truly home for the first time since she'd lost her parents.

"We're getting married as soon as I can arrange it."

She grinned, more than agreeable to any terms he wanted. "Any Sunday."

He paused and looked deep into her misty, diamond-bright eyes, letting her words sink in. "Your promotion?"

Marjorie nodded and started to say more when Lydia burst into her office.

Her friend's mouth dropped open as she stopped abruptly. "Oh . . . hi."

"Hi," Marjorie answered for them.

Lydia casually swung her arm toward Sam and Marjorie. "Have you two patched things up?"

"It's either that, or we have a peculiar way of arguing," Sam answered, and chuckled softly.

Lydia's outstretched hand fell to her side. "Well, are you two getting married or what?"

"We're getting married."

It looked for a moment as though she doubted them. "When?" she asked speculatively.

Sam and Marjorie shared a lingering look. "Any Sunday," they answered in unison.

* * * * *

Silhouette Special Edition

THE O'HURLEYS! — CHANTEL'S STORY

from
Nora Roberts

Skin Deep

Available September 1988

The third in an exciting new series about the lives and loves of triplet sisters—

In May's *The Last Honest Woman* (SE #451), Abby finally met a man she could trust . . . then tried to deceive him to protect her sons.

In July's *Dance to the Piper* (SE #463), it took some very fancy footwork to get reserved recording mogul Reed Valentine dancing to effervescent Maddy's tune. . . .

In *Skin Deep* (SE #475), find out what kind of heat it takes to melt the glamorous Chantel's icy heart. Available in September.

Silhouette Romance

COMING NEXT MONTH

#604 TYLER—Diana Palmer
Most men frightened shy Nell Regan, but her new ranch foreman,
Tyler Jacobs, was different. Could his gentle strength unlock her
heart's secret passion? LONG, TALL TEXANS TRILOGY—Book
Three!

#605 GOOD VIBRATIONS—Curtiss Ann Matlock
Stumbling on her treadmill of stress and tension, uptight Jillian
Aldritt met happy-go-lucky beach boy Max Jensen. And in Max's
arms, she tasted a freedom she'd never dreamed of....

#606 O'DANIEL'S PRIDE—Susan Haynesworth
Feisty Lera O'Daniel was struggling to save her family's farm. Times
were hard... until dashing Miles Macklin came along. Could he be
the answer to Lera's prayers?

#607 THE LOVE BANDIT—Beverly Terry
When reporter Hester Arlen interviewed the infamous Love Bandit,
she didn't expect to fall for his charms. Could a man who broke so
many hearts give his to Hester?

#608 TRUE BLISS—Barbara Turner
Trade negotiator Matthew Morgan thought big business held the
ultimate high-stakes excitement—until dazzling Bliss Kellaway blazed
into his life and showed him love had the highest stakes of all.

#609 COME BE MY LOVE—Annette Broadrick
When lawyer Gregory Duncan escaped to his friend's secluded chalet
for a much-needed rest, he didn't bargain on meeting Brandi Martin,
an irresistible woman—who desperately needed his help....

AVAILABLE THIS MONTH:

ATTRACTIVE, SPACE SAVING BOOK RACK

Display your most prized novels on this handsome and sturdy book rack. The hand-rubbed walnut finish will blend into your library decor with quiet elegance, providing a practical organizer for your favorite hard-or soft-covered books.

Only $9.95

Approximately 16" x 8" when assembled

Assembles in seconds!

Silhouette Romance

LONG, TALL TEXANS

A Trilogy by Diana Palmer

Bestselling Diana Palmer has rustled up three rugged heroes in a trilogy sure to lasso your heart! The titles of the books are your introduction to these unforgettable men:

CALHOUN

In June, you met Calhoun Ballenger. He wanted to protect Abby Clark from the world, but could he protect her from himself?

JUSTIN

Calhoun's brother, Justin—the strong, silent type—had a second chance with the woman of his dreams, Shelby Jacobs, in August.

TYLER

October's long, tall Texan is Shelby's virile brother, Tyler, who teaches shy Nell Regan to trust her instincts—especially when they lead her into his arms!

Don't miss TYLER, the last of three gripping stories from Silhouette Romance!